kiss

ONCE IS NEVER ENOUGH

Her heart slammed to a stop.

That was no toe in the pool. No testing the waters or even taking a tentative dip. It was a full-on, feel-the-rush, blast down the water slide, total body immersion into the deep end. And the most frightening thing about it was, as she peered into those brilliant blues...it was tempting as hell.

Where was her friend Maeve when she needed her most!

When she wanted someone skilled in the art of justification and adventurous enough—

And then it struck her. She didn't need Maeve at all. Not only did she know with one-hundred-percent certainty what her friend would want her to do...she knew herself.

This guy was the simple pleasure she'd been missing. He had a connection to and was obviously liked by nearly half the people at the party—so chances were good he wasn't a serial killer. This was the first time she'd met him—so chances were even better this could be something brief. Something quick.

Something in the moment.

Something she wanted more with every second that passed.

A slow smile spread to her lips.

"Okay, Blue-eyes. Let's go."

DEAR READER,

Confession time. I've become something of a *KISS*ing bandit over these past months.

That's right. A total book tart.

But with the offering of titles from Harlequin's new line, KISS, how can you blame me? I'm hooked on the fresh and the flirt. The sweet and the smolder. The heroines I want to invite over to share my chocolate and wine with. And the heroes I just *want*...because, seriously, how could I not!

These are stories I relate to. Characters I love. And books I can't get enough of.

So as much as I savor each new KISS title, once I hit that last incredible page and have my so satisfying HEA in hand...it doesn't take more than a day before I'm batting my lashes at the next month's offering, shamelessly counting down the days until I get my next KISS.

Are you enjoying the new Harlequin KISS line as much as I am?

Find me on Facebook at
www.facebook.com/MiraLynKelly.Author
or Twitter at www.twitter.com/miralynkelly
and let me know!

All my best,

Mira Lyn Kelly

ONCE IS
NEVER ENOUGH

MIRA LYN KELLY

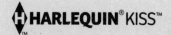

Recycling programs
for this product may
not exist in your area.

ISBN-13: 978-0-373-20721-3

ONCE IS NEVER ENOUGH

www.Harlequin.com

ABOUT MIRA LYN KELLY

Mira Lynn Kelly grew up in the Chicago area and earned her degree in fine arts from Loyola University. She met the love of her life while studying abroad in Rome, Italy, only to discover he'd been living right around the corner from her for the previous two years. Having spent her twenties working and playing in the Windy City, she's now settled with her husband in rural Minnesota, where their four beautiful children provide an excess of action, adventure and entertainment.

With writing as her passion and inspiration striking at the most unpredictable times, Mira can always be found with a notebook at the ready. (More than once the neighbors have caught her, covered in grass clippings, scribbling away atop the compost container!)

When she isn't reading, writing or running to keep up with the kids, she loves watching movies, blabbing with the girls and cooking with her husband and friends. Check out her website, www.miralynkelly.com, for the latest dish!

Other Harlequin® KISS™ titles by Mira Lyn Kelly:
Waking Up Married

This and other titles by Mira Lyn Kelly are available in ebook format. Check out **www.Harlequin.com**.

To my brilliant, hilarious, talented, sweet,
beautiful and more-fun-than-fiction children.
You are my real life Happily Ever Afters. I love you.

ONCE IS
NEVER ENOUGH

PROLOGUE

———

"So you take your reckless adventuring like you take your coffee: lukewarm and watered down?"

Nichole Daniels stared first at the *shu mai* being jabbed in dumpling accusation from across their small table, and then at the gleaming blue eyes centering her best friend's face beyond. "*Hypothetical* reckless adventuring. And, for clarification, I want to enjoy my coffee. Not get hurt by it. So I take it hot, but not scalding. I like it brewed strong, but cut with something creamy to avoid heartburn."

Maeve snorted. "You cut it with skim milk. Cripes! The whole point of this was to embrace the no-consequences element of a fantasy we weren't planning to live out. I mean, seriously, I don't want to be trapped on a deserted island at all. And if I actually was, I'd hope it would be with some kind of mechanical genius who played survival games of the non-cannibal variety in his spare time. But for the purpose of this chatty lunchtime game girlfriends play...in a context *separate* from reality...for one single night without consequences maybe you'd want something *robust*...rich... Oh, my God...something topped with whipped cream!"

"Enough, enough." Nichole laughed, cutting into Maeve's ramping excitement before the whole restaurant started staring at them. "I get the concept. Honestly, I'm just not interested."

Maeve narrowed her eyes. "It's a *fantasy*. How can you not be interested?"

Echoes of a distant conversation teased through Nichole's mind—accusations and blame, heartbreak and humiliation, and the fantasy she'd bet her future on revealed for the nightmare it was. Everything she'd lost. *Everyone.*

She'd been down that road. Twice already. No thanks for a third.

It didn't pay to pretend. Not even over a *dim sum* lunch with her best friend.

"I'm just not," she managed through a stiff smile.

"Hence your overnight-on-a-deserted-island order for a male of unspecified looks who's safe, honest and can keep up his end of a conversation." Another jab of the chopsticks. *"Lame."*

"Not lame. Maybe my reality is everything I want it to be. How about that? I've got a kickass career, a button-cute place in a cool neighborhood and the greatest friends in the world," she said, batting her eyes at the best of them. "What more could a girl ask for?"

"Do you want me to start down at the toes or up at the head... Or should I just start in the middle, 'cause that region might make my point a little faster."

"None of the above! Now, stop taunting me with your dumpling or I'm going to eat it."

Maeve snapped her chopsticks back, popping the shrimp bundle into her mouth with a grin. On finishing the bite, though, her look became more contemplative than teasing. "I'm serious, Nikki. It's been three years. Don't you ever get lonely?"

Nichole stared back, the word *no* poised on her tongue. Only as the seconds stretched, the single word that was the lie she'd been telling herself for all too long suddenly wouldn't form. Her life was so *right*—in all the ways that mattered—she hadn't let herself think too much about those times when the stillness of her apartment left a sort of hollow feeling deep in her chest. Or when the empty chair across her table kept her from using the bay window breakfast nook that was half the reason she'd signed the lease in the first place. But they were there, nonetheless, apparently lying in wait for the right opportunity to glare at her.

Maeve slumped back in her chair. "I should have given you the last *shu mai*."

"Please, it's not so dire as that," she assured her, starting to stack the plates cluttering the table. "I'm just not interested in another relationship."

"But what about—?"

The strains of Van Halen's "Hot for Teacher" cut in, signaling a call from Maeve's brother.

Hallelujah.

With Maeve scheduled to leave town for business the next day, Garrett Carter would probably keep her on the line for the next twenty minutes, reassuring himself she wouldn't leave the coffeepot on, let anyone—*anyone*—into her hotel room, or accept candy from strangers in general. Only the reprieve proved short-lived when Maeve thumbed the call through to voicemail.

Nichole reached for her wine as an unholy gleam lit her friend's eyes.

"I should set you up with Garrett."

The crisp, fruity vintage burned like acid as it hit her sinuses. Napkin to her mouth, lungs wrestling to expel the alcohol in exchange for oxygen, she choked out a strangled, "What?" Then, wheezing, "I *thought* you were my friend."

"I was thinking maybe you could learn something from him."

"Like what? The most effective antibiotics for treating—?"

"Hey." Maeve cut her off with a stern glance. "Uncalled for. He's not so bad."

Nichole cocked a brow at her. "They call him *The Panty Whisperer.* I've seen his name on the ladies' room wall. And my mother warned me about men like him."

Maeve chuckled, a sisterly combination of worship and irritation filling her eyes. "You could be dating Attila the Hun and your mother would be delirious with the whole breathless 'he's so powerful' business. Trust me, she'd take Garrett with open arms."

Nichole shook her head, knowing it was true.

"And, between you and me, Mary Newton wrote that on the wall to get even with him for putting her off when she offered up the goods. I know you've never met him, but Garrett's actually a pretty decent guy."

"'Domineering, hypocritical, arrogant, womanizing, workaholic control freak.' Gee, where did I hear that from, I wonder?"

Maeve shook her head. "Okay, take it easy. I'm not serious about setting you up. And even if I were he wouldn't go out with you. He's got a rule about dating his sisters' friends."

Handy. Because Nichole had a similar rule. She'd lost enough friends because of broken relationships. People she'd already considered family—

Fingers snapped in front of her face. "Chill! I told you I was kidding."

The muscles down her back relaxed. "Your point, then?"

"Just this. Maybe it's time to dip a toe back into the dating pool. Test the waters and see how it goes. I know in the past your relationships have always been... serious. But they don't have to be. Look, Garrett's the only guy I know as commitment-phobic as you. But you can bet *he* isn't lonely. He's proof positive a couple of dates for the sake of some non-platonic company can be just that—a couple of dates. Simple. No big deal."

Yeah, except the last time Nichole had gone on "a

couple of dates" she ended up with a white dress she'd never worn, thousands blown on non-refundable deposits, the very fabric of her life torn asunder and an aversion to fantasies and forever powerful enough to keep her out of romance for three years running.

As it turned out, that fateful "it's not me, it's you" speech had been the best thing ever to happen to her.

She'd been lucky to escape a marriage that, despite what she'd believed at the time, would have been a train wreck. Lucky to have chosen Chicago as the city to clean slate her life in. And luckiest of all to have picked the open treadmill next to Maeve's that Friday that had, in essence, been the first day of the rest of Nichole's new life.

She hadn't been tempted to even the merest flirtation since. Not once. And she honestly couldn't imagine that changing anytime soon.

But, seeing Maeve about to come at her from another angle, Nichole held up a staying hand. "How about this. If I happen to meet someone who actually makes it hard to say no, I promise I'll give Garrett a call to talk me through The Panty Whisperer's six-step guide to keeping it casual—"

"Ha-ha. Very funny," Maeve grumbled, flagging the waitress for their check.

"But until then I'm not dipping my toe in anything."

ONE

—

Good Lord, was that a tongue?

Nichole Daniels ripped her attention from the kiss deepening at exponential rates less than fifty feet away and dragged it back to where Chicago's cityscape reflected the molten hues of the western sky.

Having arrived early to help her friend Sam set up for his rooftop bash to welcome his older brother home from Europe, she'd been stocking wash pails with beer, wine and a myriad other pre-packaged cocktails when the lovebirds had pushed out the door, their breathless laughter dying at the sight of her. With the party scheduled to start—well, right then, for the few minutes before the guests migrated up to the terrace she'd figured the roof would be big enough for the three of them. Only now the evening breeze had picked up, carrying with it whispers not meant for her ears. Private words and promises of the kind of forever she'd stopped dreaming about years ago. The intimacy of their exchange had her feeling like some kind of creepy voyeur.

Boxing up the last packaging to recycle, she eyed the door. Anytime now...

People always showed up early for Sam's parties. The view from his roof was one of the best in the city for watching the sunset.

A muffled groan.

Awkward.

Tipping the longneck that hung from her fingers for a small draw of the lemony draft, she glanced down at her phone for the hundredth time. She saw a text from her mother, who was checking to see if she had any *special* plans for the night, so she pushed it aside on the picnic tabletop, making a mental note to call her the next day.

Tonight she wasn't in the mood for a diatribe on beggars versus choosers, ticking clocks and doing the work to make her dreams a reality. No matter how well-intentioned her mother might be, a guilt-flavored pep-talk wasn't on the evening's agenda.

Another gasp. This one edged with unmistakable need—and she hazarded a sidelong glance—

Whoa! Mistake!

She *hadn't* just seen...and the hands...and the legs...

Jumping clumsily from the picnic table, Nichole stumbled back and made a beeline for the stairway access.

Eyes on the ground. Eyes. On. The. Ground.

She was halfway down the narrow flight, ready to

text Maeve her first report from the party, when she stopped, staring blankly at her open, empty palm.

She'd left her phone.

Her stomach turned to lead as she hesitantly looked back up to the roof. The sunset she could live without. But that phone was her lifeline. All her contacts... appointments...shopping lists...music...*Maeve*.

She had to go back. Only she *really* didn't want to.

Maybe if she gave it a minute or two they'd be done and she'd be able to collect her phone without feeling like she needed to boil her eyes in bleach or start therapy seven days a week to scrub the memory from her mind.

How long had it been already? She didn't even know. So accustomed to her pretty little pink-rubber-clad smartphone, who needed a watch?

Okay, this was ridiculous. She was an adult, and her phone was a critical part of her existence. She turned toward the roof, bottom lip parked between her teeth, foot poised to advance—

The door below opened and she glanced back, hoping against hope it was Sam so she could make *him* get the darned phone for her. Only this wasn't her five-foot-ten-if-she-looked-up-just-right, whipcord-thin blond bud, come to rescue her phone, but rather a six-foot-something stranger in worn jeans and a white Oxford rolled back at the arms, shouldering through a doorway made too small by his frame.

Head bowed, he called back to someone within the apartment, "Yeah, see you up there in a few."

Maybe she should warn the guy about the rooftop action. Only before she could figure quite how to phrase it, the head topped with short, disheveled, dark curls tipped back, revealing a set of electric blue eyes that sent a shock straight through the center of her. Her mind whirled and stalled as recognition washed over her in a wave, receding just as quickly.

She'd have sworn she knew him.

"Looks like we had the same idea to catch the sunset," he offered with an easy smile and a jut of his chin toward the roof as he took the steps at a loose jog, meeting her at the midpoint of the stairwell. "You going up?"

"I think I have to," she answered weakly, her eyes tracking nervously to the rectangle of open sky at the top of the stairs. "I left my phone when I ran...."

Her phone would be fine. It wasn't like she'd left it balancing on the rail.

Was it possible they were finished?

"Ran?"

Of course it was possible. Probable? Who knew?

"Did something happen up there?"

"Yeah," she answered with a shudder as she covered her eyes with her hands. The way they'd started going at it—she'd never seen...never done....

Heat penetrated the fog of her embarrassed shock, radiating from a concentrated point where his hand, wide and heavy, covered her shoulder in a reassuring squeeze. "Go down to Sam. Stay with him."

And then he was bypassing her on the narrow stairwell, somehow managing to keep all that brawn from doing more than warming the scant space between them. The proximity was unnerving, distracting her even more than the scene she'd witnessed on the rooftop...where this guy was heading...his every step landing like an increasing threat.

Wait. *Did something happen?*

Oh...*no.*

Her breath caught.

Oh, no.

"Oh, no! Wait," she gasped, realizing too late what he'd been asking her.

The eyes that looked back at her as his steps continued were anything but laughing. "Go downstairs. I'll take care of this guy."

Take care of—? She watched his retreating back expand impossibly, blotting out the light of the evening sky beyond. "No, really," she yelped, scrambling up the steps behind him. "You—um—blue-eyed guy—wait!"

But he just held a staying hand behind him as he hit the open access to the rooftop. At best this was about to get extremely embarrassing for both of them. She had to do something—and fast.

"Sex!"

Oh, God, that hadn't come out right either. Except the guy's steps slowed and his head cranked around, revealing all that deep blue intensity replaced with confusion. "Excuse me?"

She raced up the stairs behind him, heart pounding—though not due to any sort of exertion from the short flight. Heck, she and Maeve could run a half-marathon on the treadmill if they had a season of *Game of Thrones* playing in front of them. Her heart had hit double-time due to embarrassment and a desperate need to stop this really protective guy before he tossed someone off the side of the roof.

Swallowing hard, one hand waving around, she looked for a salvation that wasn't coming. Finally she looked at him apologetically. "They were sort of having sex up there. That's what happened. I'm sorry... and...um...thank you too—I think."

She'd never seen eyes change in so many ways in such a short span of time. But this guy's were like a visual aid for defining "window to the soul." Everything was right there within them. Shock, relief, amusement, and then a slow-growing interest that tugged at some long-forgotten place inside her.

Something she shook off without more than a second's consideration.

A fractured cry of the climactic variety split the air between them, setting her cheeks to blaze like the sky beyond.

"Damn," was his only response, and something about the smacked look on his face struck her as ridiculously funny within the awkwardness of the moment.

"Yeah." She laughed, covering her ears. "You're telling me. I think we ought to give them some privacy... but I really need my phone. I'll bake you a cake if you'll get it for me."

Maeve would bake the cake. If she'd been here, none of this would have happened.

"Cake?"

"Please?"

"I'm a tough customer when it comes to cake. My sisters have spoiled me pretty bad. How about this? You go grab your phone and I'll take care of Team Romance behind us."

This guy didn't know what he was missing. But if Blue Eyes didn't want Maeve's baking...? Fine with her. This way she got her sunset, her phone and a cake too. Because, now that she was thinking about it, Maeve was *definitely* going to make her one when she got back in town. "Deal."

An awkward moment, many murmured apologies and some quiet shuffling later, her defender of public decency stepped up to the rail beside her, resting his forearms over the worn wood as he squinted into the sinking sun. "I'll admit I was half tempted to pull out a pencil and start taking notes."

Nichole shook her head, unable to fight the pull at the corner of her mouth.

"What? I would have given you a copy. Though maybe too early for that kind of kink in our relationship?"

Coughing out a laugh, she leaned back, forcibly resisting the draw to lean closer. "Yeah, you're probably right."

"Based on that pretty blush, I'd say definitely. So how about it, Red? Sun's going down fast."

"Red?" she asked, mildly disappointed by the moniker that had followed her around half her life. For some unaccountable reason she'd thought—hoped?—no, that couldn't be right—this guy might be different.

"Blue-eyed guy?" he challenged back, then tapped a finger to his cheek while nodding at hers. "Red."

For her blush, not her hair.

Such a small distinction, and yet big enough to push a smile to her lips as she followed his gaze to the burned amber glow of the pooling sun. It was beautiful. And, with the mellow notes of Jack Johnson filtering the rush of city traffic rising from the streets below, peaceful.

For long moments they watched, remaining quiet until the last molten drop bled beneath the horizon.

Forearms resting over the rail, muscular back rounded beneath the pull of his shirt, the familiar stranger beside her let out a long, deeply contented breath.

"Wow. That good, huh?" she asked teasingly, anxious to relieve the unsettling intimacy of the moment.

Casting her a sidelong glance, he considered. Then, pushing back to straighten, he shoved his hands into his pockets and met her gaze in earnest. "Yeah, it was."

"Not a lot of time for sunsets?"

His mouth pulled to the side and his broad shoulders hunched forward. "You know, it's not that I haven't seen them. More a matter of being too caught up in everything else going on—where I've got to be next, how much needs to get done, what all's about to get away from me." He shook his head, a frown darkening his gaze as it held hers. "Been a long time since I've been able to slow down and just...enjoy the simple stuff. Too long."

A few plainly spoken words. Nothing particularly deep. And yet the way he'd said them—as though making a reluctant admission—gave them power enough to penetrate the superficial and resonate within her.

"I get it. The little things have a way of passing you by pretty quickly if you aren't paying attention. And then, when you finally notice, sometimes all you've missed doesn't exactly feel so small."

"Yeah, that's about it." He laughed then—a brusque, dismissive sound—but even as he did so those deep blue eyes held hers with an almost questioning intensity. "So what's been passing you by?"

Maybe just this.

She should have looked away. Made light of the two of them standing there. Thrown out a joke or an excuse to put some space between them. Only for the first time in three years she didn't want the space or the buffer of meaningless banter. She wanted to stretch the moment and all the simplicity it offered—make it last for the both of them.

That was crazy. She didn't know this guy. Didn't know anything more than that he'd made some vague reference to a busy life and the desire not to miss out on the simple stuff. And yet there was something about him—an odd sense of familiarity, connection— that made her feel like she did. Made her think about her own life and the simple things she avoided out of fear for the complications they could bring.

"That much, huh?" he asked, breaking into her thoughts with a reminder she hadn't answered. Laugh lines creased the skin around his eyes as he cocked his head to the side. "Looks like we could both use a few more sunsets."

"Looks like," she agreed, all too grateful for the simple reprieve.

Damn, there it was again. That hot red rising to the surface of her skin. Betraying the woman beneath in all the best ways. He couldn't get enough, and it was taking the bulk of his restraint not to work her pretty blush for everything it was worth.

But he hadn't come to Jesse's welcome-home party to pick someone up. In fact finding a woman had been the last thing on his mind.

He'd wanted to go out. Reconnect with friends. Watch a sunset.

After six years of walking through his front door with half his takeout already consumed and heading straight to his back office—where, on a good day, he'd be able to set aside one kind of work for another—he was done. And now, degree in hand, he wanted the straightforward simplicity of knowing he'd put his day to bed and the night was his...finally...to do with as he pleased.

But there she'd been. Looking lost. And, damn, he hadn't known what. Having raised his four sisters through their teens, he found his mind had a way of going to dark places pretty fast when he didn't understand what was happening. Thank God he'd been wrong. Only by the time he'd understood where all that vulnerability was coming from—the mad make-out scene which even *he* had to admit had been pretty intense—she'd made his radar. Registered as more than a collection of pleasing physical attributes falling under the category of female.

And then she'd been standing there, backlit by the cooling sky, looking into his eyes with that thoughtful kind of amazement in hers telling him she *got* him. Making him wonder if maybe she did.

"Well, would you look what the cat dragged in?" came the first of several raucous calls, derailing his train of thought as a group of the old crew jogged up to the rooftop.

"Sam said you were here, man, but I didn't dare believe."

"Dude! No way."

Laughing brown eyes peered up at him. "All this is for you?"

"So it would seem," he answered, with a wide grin at seeing so many of the old faces he'd lost touch with. "It's been a while."

"Too long?" she asked, a mirthful smile playing across her lips.

"Definitely too long."

Just then her phone sounded and, holding it up

with a little wave, she started to back away. "I'll let you catch up, then."

He reached for her elbow. Followed her gaze as it slipped to the point of contact between them, lingered and then returned almost tentatively to his.

"Thanks for the sunset, Red."

"You too, Blue Eyes," she offered quietly, backing away as he withdrew his hand, before she took the stairs down to Sam's apartment.

A solid clap on his shoulder pulled him back to the guys, the laughter, greetings and jibes.

"Damn, Garrett. What are you? Here fifteen minutes and already you've got the next victim cued up and ready to go. I bow to you, dude."

Garrett Carter looked back at the guys he'd gone to high school with and shook his head.

Aw, hell. Not this again.

TWO

—

Phone clutched to her ear, Nichole stopped in the quiet alcove at the bottom of the stairwell, her heart thumping in her chest. "I think I dipped a toe back in the pool."

"Wait—what? You think—" Maeve's distracted voice was cut off as her breath was sucked in. "Shut it! You didn't... Oh, my God—tell. *Tell!*"

Nichole hadn't gotten more than a few sentences in when Maeve interrupted.

"Stop, stop, stop. Set the stage, for crying out loud. Details. And, so you don't waste my time with a lot of trash about the temperature or the number of cigarette butts around the roof, I'm talking about the guy. Hotness ranking. The good kind of dirty or clean-cut? Build and bulk. Distinguishing features. Height. You get the idea. Don't skimp. Then get to the good toe-dipping stuff... Damn it, *why* am I in Denver?"

Nichole pulled the phone from her ear and looked at it, suddenly wishing she'd thought to Skype. Maeve sounded like she hadn't slept in two days and Nichole figured the look on her face as she shot off her rapid fire laundry list of must-know information would be priceless.

"Easy, Maeve." She laughed into the phone, stepping clear as a large group edged past her, heading for the roof. "How are negotiations on the deal going?"

"The guy, Nikki. Don't make me beg."

"Okay, okay. So he's definitely one of those men who draws the eye. Kind of magnetic. Over six feet. More rugged than pretty. And there was something about his eyes... When this guy looks at you...I don't even know how to describe it."

"Mmhmm...mmhmm. I like it. Keep going."

Nichole shook her head and chuckled, leaning back against the wall as she laid down what physical details she could before recounting the few minutes they'd shared. When she'd finished, Maeve let out an indelicate cough.

"That's *it*? What part of that had your toe anywhere near the pool? It doesn't sound like you got wet at all."

Feeling slightly miffed, Nichole ignored the snicker and subtle pun to counter, "I didn't say I jumped him! It was just a really nice quiet moment that had a very different feel than when I'm hanging out with Sam or you or any of the usual crowd, for example. It wasn't going anywhere. But there was a kind of sizzly thing in the air, and it definitely had a toe-dipping feel."

Maeve was quiet a moment, then asked. "So, if there was sizzle, why wouldn't it go anywhere?"

"Hold on a sec." Nichole pressed further into the wall behind her, waving quick hellos to a stream of partygoers heading up to the roof. After the stairwell was cleared, she answered, "I don't think he's even from around here. I've never seen him before. But he knows a bunch of guys I think must be Jesse's friends. I kind of got the feeling he was visiting from out of town."

"Hmm... So let's recap. You've got an aversion to commitment. You've met a ruggedly hot hunk with whom you share 'sizzle' and you think he's just in town for a visit. It feels like there ought to be an obvious solution here. Like maybe you could have your hunk and eat hi—"

"That's enough," she cut in, feeling a renewed burn in her cheeks. "I get what you're saying. But, no. Seriously, just no."

Maeve's sigh was long suffering, and even longer drawn out, but Nichole could hear the smile behind it.

"Fine. Waste this perfectly good opportunity for what sounds like some simple fun without a whole lot of strings."

Nichole's brows drew down and her gaze slid up to the rooftop doorway.

No. It had been a couple of minutes. A fleeting kind of connection. That was all.

Another larger group filed past. Following them up, she wrapped her call with Maeve, promising more gossip and snaps from the party as available.

On the roof, Nichole glanced around at what had

become a dense crowd. With the way people were pouring into the place now she probably wouldn't even see him again. Which was good. Because she really wasn't interested.

Though even as she thought it, she realized she was scanning faces. Her gaze slipping past friends and acquaintances without stopping in an absent-minded search for the stranger who was making a liar out of her even as she stood there.

And then she found him. Nearly a head taller than most everyone around him. That vivid blue gaze locked steadily with hers.

A loud cheer sounded and all attention shifted to the doorway. Jesse had jogged up and was standing with a stunned grin on his face. She'd only met him once before he'd left, two years ago, but she remembered him to be as cool as his brother, who was now pulling him in for a solid hug.

She looked back to where her blue-eyed hero had been a moment before, but within the shifting crowd she'd lost him.

The party was in full swing, the roof packed to capacity, the atmosphere as welcoming as Jesse and Sam's ever-expanding social network. Garrett had managed to get a couple of minutes with his oldest friend and to secure plans for later in the week before letting the next eager guest at him. He hadn't been two feet out of the crush before finding *her* again.

Nichole. That was her name. It had taken him the

better part of an hour to pick it out from a nearby conversation, roll it around in his mind and connect it to the woman with the glittering almond eyes and fiery spill of curls, the long legs in dark jeans and the strappy little top with the tiny bow.

Standing within a loose grouping of friends and acquaintances of whom they both seemed to know some, but not all, they'd been talking around each other for hours now. Much as they'd been circling throughout the night. Picking up hints through rapid banter interspersed with old stories and private jokes. Exchanging looks that, within their lifespan of a scant handful of seconds, said more than all the words they'd shared combined...and then moving on.

Only now all those hints, bits and pieces had begun to take shape in his mind, forming the image of a woman he liked. A woman who laughed easily, spoke intelligently and didn't take herself too seriously. A woman who liked to joke and tease. Who gave as good as she got. And whose unconscious smile did something to him he couldn't quite put a name to.

He wanted her.

Not the way he usually wanted his dates. Not for some superficial conversation and perfunctory dinner or drinks that were the means to an end he'd been limiting himself to for as long as he could remember. All he'd had time for. All he could afford. Because he'd spent every spare minute he had on making his construction company top in the city, earning his degree and keeping his four sisters from doing all the things he didn't want them to do.

Nichole made him want more. She made him curious. Made him want to linger. To take his time and find out if maybe they could have something...uncomplicated. Casual, but real. For a while.

He wanted the rest too. The parts where he pushed that pretty blush to see how deep and dark and far it could spread. The parts where he had her beneath him, all that fiery red hair wrapped around his fists and spilling over his pillow as he pushed inside her body. But when those parts were over, and before they even began, he wanted more. And he wanted it soon.

Laughter subsiding, Nichole sighed, her dark gaze finding his beneath the ashy fringe of her lashes. It wasn't coy or contrived. Nor the blatant invitation he'd lost interest in back in his twenties. It was contemplative. Heated, but questioning. Enticing in its hint of uncertainty.

Damn, if that didn't make her all the better.

Around them the conversation had somehow found its way to movies filmed in Chicago and who could name the most. Beneath the titles volleying back and forth, Garrett gave a subtle nod of his head toward the quiet corner of the rooftop where they'd watched the sunset.

Nichole's slender brows drew together, her teeth setting into her lush bottom lip in the ultimate expression of uncertainty.

It shouldn't have gone straight to his groin, but it

did. At least until he saw her fooling with that phone she carried around. One thumb brushed the smooth screen and—was she...*texting?*

Immediately he thought of his sister, "using a lifeline" to make some inane decision she didn't trust him enough to help her with. Was that what this was? Indecision over whether to step over to a corner and *talk* with him?

Sure, he had every intention of taking it further, but for now—

Wait... What the hell...? She was *not* holding that phone up to take his picture.

Eyes on the screen, only half listening to an escalating debate over whether the outlying suburbs and thus the John Hughes classics counted, Nichole had been trying to frame the shot when her subject was suddenly front and center—closer than he'd been edging past her down in the access stairwell.

Oh, God. She'd been busted taking his picture to send to Maeve. This was an all-time low.

Her gaze crawling up the towering expanse of Oxford cloth and then creeping over the tantalizing stretch of bare masculine skin at the base of his neck, she forced herself to keep going until she reached the now steely blue of his eyes. Her stomach tumbled into free fall.

"What're you doing, Red?"

Swallowing past the tight knot in her throat, she shook her head.

What *was* she doing? Trying to snap a picture of some virtual stranger because she couldn't account for the reaction she was having to him? Because she couldn't keep her eyes off him for more than three seconds at a stretch and she needed the judgment of a reliable outside source? Someone who knew her just about as well as she knew herself. Maeve.

So, basically, she was acting like a complete nut-job.

And yet a part of her still twitched with the need to get a photo and hit "send." It must have been obvious too, because seconds later a hand firmed around her wrist—loose, but uncompromising—and pushed the phone down to her side.

The skin beneath his grasp warmed as though a low charge ran from his hand up through hers. It felt good. Too good. And suddenly all she could think about was how long it had been since anyone had touched her for more than the briefest instant. What a simple pleasure that heated, lingering contact was. And how she hadn't even realized she missed it.

He was bending close to her ear and his breath washed warm across skin that seemed to come alive beneath it. "Red?"

The air went thin around her as the slow tingle behind her ear began to spread, sliding down her neck, shoulder and arm until it came to mingle with the charge emanating from her wrist.

"I don't know what I'm doing. Men don't usually— I mean, I don't—" Trying to find the words, she licked her lips, watched his eyes darken at the sight. "There's something about you."

Maybe it was the way he hadn't hesitated to protect a woman he didn't know. Or how he was built like he pounded rocks for a living but could argue international economics as easily as the merits of Leia over Uhura. How he savored opportunities to stop and enjoy the simple stuff. Or how his offbeat jokes made her laugh like she'd known him forever.

Or maybe it was just that when his gaze drifted to her hair, she could *feel* his fingers tightening in it.

Could it be so simple? He made her feel like a woman and made her notice him as a man...when for so long no one else had.

A gravel-rough laugh rumbled from low in his chest and the hand at her wrist loosened, easing into a slow up and down caress over the bare skin of her arm. "There's something about you too. So what do you say to getting out of here and figuring out just what it is?"

Getting out of here? Her heart slammed to a stop.

That was no toe in the pool. No testing the waters or even taking a tentative dip. It was a full-on, feel-the-rush blast down a water slide—total body immersion into the deep end. And the most frightening thing about it was...as she peered into those brilliant blues... it was tempting as hell.

Where was Maeve when she needed her most?

When she wanted someone skilled in the art of justification and adventurous enough to—?

And then it struck her. She didn't need Maeve at

all. Not only did she know with one-hundred-percent certainty what her friend would want her to do...she knew herself.

This guy was the simple pleasure she'd been missing. He had a connection to and was obviously liked by nearly half the people at the party—so chances were good he wasn't a serial killer. This was the first time she'd met him, and from what she'd gathered he didn't live in the area but up north somewhere—so chances were even better this could be something brief. Something quick.

Something in the moment.

Something she wanted more with every second that passed.

A slow smile spread to her lips.

"Okay, Blue Eyes. Let's go."

THREE

—

"Let's go."

Garrett had known even before the words left her mouth. He'd seen the way those soft brown eyes steadied, sensed the change in the air between them, and had felt his own body respond to the first victory.

A quick scan of the rooftop confirmed at least half a dozen sets of eyes on them. Not what he would have preferred, but there was nothing to be done about it now.

"Yeah, let's go." Taking her hand, he kept his eyes on hers as they headed toward the stairwell. If she was looking at him she wouldn't notice the raised brows, wouldn't worry about the quiet snickers, wouldn't think about anything but finding a place where they could talk. *To* each other instead of *around* each other. There'd used to be a coffee house in the neighborhood he'd heard was pretty popular for the late-night crowd. Perhaps it was time to find out for himself.

At the bottom of the stairs Nichole stopped. "Do you need to say goodbye to anyone?"

"Nah, I'm good." He'd call Jesse tomorrow. The rest of the guys he'd see soon enough. "You?"

Her mouth pulled to the side as she shook her head and glanced away.

"Are you worried about people seeing us leave together?" He hoped like hell that wasn't it. While his returning to the party alone would possibly minimize it, most likely the damage was already done.

"I'm twenty-six, not sixteen." She laughed, sounding more nervous, he was sure, than she'd intended. "It's just that I'm acting a little out of character here and I don't want to lose my nerve."

Damn, she was cute. He rubbed his thumb in a light circle over her knuckle and leaned in conspiratorially. "Lose your nerve for what?"

He'd asked it as a taunt, finding her all too easy to tease and loving the fast rise of red to her cheeks. Only when she turned, head tipping back as her gaze lifted to his, the wild blush he'd been hoping for wasn't anywhere to be found. Instead a sort of uncertain determination lit her face, making him wonder just what she was struggling with.

Brushing a stray curl from her brow, he caught the quick dart of a pink tongue across the swell of her bottom lip, felt the pull of this thing between them tugging him closer, making him want to take advantage of the empty stairwell, the dim lighting and the mouth that was driving him to distraction.

He needed to get her out of there. Into his b—

No. Not yet. This one was different.

Those soulful brown eyes searched his, the lingering intimacy fraying the tether of his restraint. The soft press of her body against his, unraveling his control.

"My nerve for this," she murmured, her breath a fluttery rush against his skin an instant before she kissed him—pressed her mouth to his and tasted his lips with the barest flick of her tongue, demolishing the man he'd wanted to be for her and giving rise to the man she'd invited in.

Hell.

Tucking the hand still holding hers at the small of her back, he drew a slow breath at that most enticing spot just below a woman's ear. Let her quiet shudder and sweet scent flood his senses and wreak havoc on his body.

"That's what you want?" he asked in a low growl, knowing it was but wanting to hear her say it just the same.

"I've been worried about avoiding complications so long I think maybe I've been missing a lot of the simple stuff too." She swallowed, heat pouring off her as she finished, "I don't want to miss this."

She couldn't get any better. "Then you won't."

Ten minutes later, amid gasps of laughter and lust, Garrett turned the key and Nichole's front door swung open under the combined weight of their bodies. Spilling into her front hall, Garrett righted them both, kicked the door closed with a sweep of his leg and threw the lock. She backed across the open hardwood, barely a step ahead of him, eyes glittering, lips curved and parted as her breath came in shallow pants.

Her gaze swept the length of him and the now persistent flush of her cheeks deepened, driving the blood hard and fast to his already aching groin. Reaching for him, her slender fingers curved around his belt, pulling until he allowed her to tow him closer. Close enough that he could reach around her, cover the firm curves of her ass with his hands, slide lower still to the backs of her thighs and hoist her up against him.

Her breath caught as her ankles locked behind his back, the soft brown of her eyes going nearly black as her pupils pushed wide.

"God, you're beautiful," he groaned, fighting the urge to take her there against the wall.

Nodding distractedly, she went to work on the buttons down the front of his shirt, pushing at the panels like she was revealing Superman's emblem beneath. And when she answered, "You too," her eyes glazing at the sight of him, taking a building in a single bound didn't seem so impossible.

The door to her room was open ahead, and the sight of her neat bed with its delicate lilac print spread made him harder than he could ever remember being. Hell, yes, he was hungry for the sex. For her body. For the pretty pink that tinged her skin and the sounds she'd make when he took her over the edge. He wanted all of that. But this—this anticipation burning through his veins—was for what would come after. For the part that was going to be different. The part he would wait for until he'd wrung every moan and gasp Nichole's body had to offer out of her.

At her bed, he set her back on the mattress, supporting himself on one arm.

Legs still wrapped around his hips, she looked up at him. "I don't even know your name."

He'd opened his mouth to tell her when something in the depths of those deep dark eyes gave him pause. Something excited.

The corner of his mouth kicked up. Lowering his voice to a taunting growl, he asked, "So the question is, do you like it better that way?"

The half-moan, half-gasp that escaped her slender throat was answer enough to just about push him over the edge.

Had he actually thought she couldn't get any better?

Perfect. This hot, hard, mouthwatering male specimen was her sunset. Her uncomplicated simple pleasure. This was the fantasy she could finally afford to play out. The reckless adventure she hadn't dared to dream. And, more, it was safe.

Because she didn't even know his name.

Women didn't plan forevers around nameless men. They didn't get the wrong idea. Misinterpret intentions. Or get caught up in dreams that would take them nowhere.

They got a single night *sans* complications.

This was the one night of wild abandon she'd been unconsciously saving up for for three years. Longer than that if she was willing to look back. But she wasn't. Not tonight. Not when this moment, right now—as the familiar stranger above her lowered his mouth to the hollow between her breasts—was too good to miss even one second of.

Those blue eyes peered up at her as the corner of his mouth twisted into a mischievous smile. "This little bow here," he murmured gruffly, "has been begging me to play with it all night." Then, catching one loose string between his teeth, he tugged until the knot slipped free, taking Nichole's next breath with it.

She hadn't thought of the peach cami as particularly sexy, hadn't consciously drawn attention to herself for years. But at the rough sound of appreciation scraping from his throat as he used his hand to part the tiny expanse of soft cotton between her breasts just that much further, she flushed with the pleasure of knowing it was.

His tongue swirled deep in the hollow there, wetting the skin first and then blowing a cool breath across it after, making her belly turn and twist.

There wasn't enough contact between them. Not for the way her body was beginning to ache. To heat. To need. He was above her on the bed, his weight supported on one arm and the knees that straddled her thigh.

His tongue made another wet foray across the swell

of her breast and then stopped within a warm, teasing breath of her nipple. So close.

Arching into him, she offered the straining bud to his kiss, begging him to push her bra aside and take. But just as quickly he eased back, drawing another wet trail up to her collarbone, her neck and then to the decadent spot behind her ear that had never felt quite so sensitive as this.

"I want you naked, Nichole," he growled against the spot, making her heart skitter and pound.

"You know my name," she gasped as his palm smoothed over her belly to the hem of her shirt and pushed it up.

Pulling the gathered fabric over her head, he tossed the shirt aside and stared down at her breasts, covered in a plain cream demi-cup. "And you don't know mine."

She swallowed hard.

It shouldn't have been exciting. She only wanted to think of it as a safeguard, a defense against this man who'd stirred the first response her body had known in three years, and quite possibly the strongest ever. But there was no mistaking the playful taunt in his tone. This was sexy gameplay. Or maybe a second cousin to it. It had to be some relation based on the way the words alone and all their suggestive implications licked at the needy, achy places within her. Places she hadn't thought existed.

A flick of his finger and the front clasp opened. Another and she was bared to him. The peaks of her nipples tight and straining for a touch only he could give her. And now, watching the way that electric blue glaze zeroed in on them, she didn't think she'd manage her next breath if he didn't ease them.

"Naked, Nichole."

FOUR

—

Backing off the bed he helped her out of her jeans and panties. Staring in blatant appreciation at her naked form spread out before him, he shed his shirt with a few efficient jerks and went to work on his belt.

Nichole's mouth went dry, her eyes wide. And then she was on her knees at the edge of the bed, pushing his hands from the wide length of leather and running her own up the steep plains of his chest. She'd felt the power in his shoulders when he carried her, seen the definition across his pecs when she'd opened his shirt, but this—nothing had prepared her for the hard-cut terrain of his shirtless form.

He was like a work of art. A Greek god. A veritable playground of muscle and man. And he was only *half* undressed.

"Naked," she murmured, her fingers jumping the crest of each abdominal ridge as they descended back to his belt, tugged the stiff leather until the buckle freed, before moving on to his straining fly.

He stood patient before her as she opened his zipper with trembling fingers. As if he sensed her need to be an active participant rather than a passive player. But still he touched her all the while, never breaking contact, his hands always moving, coasting over her bare shoulders, her neck and back as she pushed the denim low on his hips. His thumbs brushed the line of her jaw, the swell of her bottom lip, the hollow at the base of her throat as she eased the stretchy waistband of his white cotton boxer briefs over the thick head of his erection and saw for the first time his actual size.

Big. Like everything else about him.

Different. Than anything she'd experienced before.

Exciting. In a way she'd never known.

Unable to resist, she closed a hand over him, testing the steely length.

"Nichole."

At the gruff sound of her name she lifted her gaze up, up, up until she met the blue burn of his. Intense. Barely contained. A shocking contrast to the light touch he'd treated her to. The look in his eyes said he wanted to throw her back on the bed and take her hard. Let the weight of his body hold her down.

Wow. Okay. She was pretty sure she wanted that too.

She gave him the space to toe off his shoes and discard his jeans, retrieving his wallet and the condom within in the process.

Breathless with mounting anticipation, she waited for him to rip it open and roll it on...frowned as he tossed it onto the bed instead.

Please don't let him be one of those guys who only wants to wear protection at the very end. She was so excited, so caught up in the magic of what was happening, the wet blanket of a conversation about risks and necessity and protection really wasn't one she wanted to need to have.

At her questioning stare, his brow quirked.

Okay—so, yes. She was going to have to have the conversation. "Umm, you're going to wear that? The whole time, right?"

The eyes above her looked briefly confused, then cleared completely. "I would never take that kind of risk, Nichole. Not with your life. Not with mine."

The conviction in his words was unmistakable, and left her with no doubt about his sincerity or commitment to their mutual protection. Which was incredibly sexy.

Almost as much as when his mouth tipped in a way that suggested a secret lingered behind his crooked smile. One he looked forward to sharing with her.

"What? You didn't think the fun and games were over yet, did you?"

She swallowed, unwilling to admit that in her experience the bulk sum of "fun and games" took place between the time the condom went on and came off. "I—I don't know."

He leaned in closer, and then closer still, so the light

pressure of his mouth against her ear and his bare chest at her shoulder guided her down to the bed. "Not even close."

Nervous laughter escaped her even as her inner walls clenched with unmet need.

His hand moved between her legs, cupping her sex as he held her gaze. A single thick finger slid between her swollen folds and then inside her. Deep and deeper. Slow and steady. He withdrew to paint a light circle around that throbbing bundle of nerves—the callused pad of a workman's finger adding sensation when she was already beyond what she'd believed she could take—his gentle, rough touch a decadent sensual contrast.

Different.

Every single thing about him.

About this night.

Another slow thrust of his finger and her hips rocked to meet him. Her back arched and the desire pooling warm and thick through her belly spilled free, making her slick, making her beg. "Please. I need—"

"You need more?" A second finger joined the first, this one pushing a gasp from her lungs instead of words.

Want coiled tight within her, making her pulse around his slow thrusts. Making her skin heat and her center burn. "I need you—"

"To make you wait? Make you so hot and ready..." the strong draw of his mouth on her nipple stole conscious thought "...that when you finally fall over the edge it'll feel like forever?"

"Oh, God." Her body seized, liquid heat scorching through her veins, pushing her fast toward the very edge he'd threatened to pull her back from. "I— I'm so close. Please—it's been so long. Please."

His touch far inside her, he met her gaze. "How long?"

Another deep thrust, this one slower, so she felt the curl of his fingers stroking, teasing some wicked spot that promised to make her its slave.

"Years," she admitted on a broken gasp, unable to bear the intensity of his stare a moment longer.

His hand stilled. Withdrew as the bed sagged under his shifting weight.

Her eyes shot open, panic slamming through her. He couldn't stop. Not now. "No, wait—"

Only then she saw he wasn't leaving the bed at all, but rather moving between her legs. His wide hands spread them apart in a way that with any other man would have left her feeling vulnerable, exposed. Not with him. Not when his big hands slid beneath her bottom and wide shoulders braced her thighs. Not when he looked into her eyes and said, "No more waiting."

And then his mouth was covering her, his tongue mimicking the actions of his fingers and hands only moments ago...only it was different. So very, incredibly different. So much more...intense. Stimulating. Hard and soft and wet and strong. Everything. He was delving inside her and then licking a path to her most sensitive spot.

Stroking.

Nibbling.

Circling with the wet velvet point of his tongue.

Making her gasp and cry and beg and scream.

And then he closed over her...drawing deep against the throbbing, needy ache. Pulling sensation from every tingling extremity...centering it all...at that one...concentrated...spot.

She was falling.

So hard. So good. So long.

Finding her release had never been so incredible. Not even close.

Maybe it was the anonymity. Or semi-anonymity anyway, since he'd made it clear he knew her name, saying it again and again in a deep, rumbling voice that stroked her every nerve like the wet tongue that spoke it.

And then he was crawling over her, giving her a taste of his body atop hers.

His lips grazed her neck. Tender. Lingering. He was going for the condom, but not in any rush. And she realized he was savoring her as he'd savored their sunset.

Oh, no. That fluttery sort of ache in her chest, making her want to link her arms around his neck and pull him closer, didn't belong there. Or maybe it did. Maybe it was just a normal side effect of endorphins being released and not her reckless heart getting ahead of her. She didn't know. What she needed was an expert. Someone with a point of reference when it came to "casual."

She couldn't even believe she was thinking it—and while she was still in bed with her blue-eyed stranger. But maybe Maeve was right and she should talk to—

"Garrett," came the gruff, deeply masculine voice from above her.

Her eyes blinked wide as the flutter in her chest dropped into her belly, turning leaden and still.

"I can feel you getting tense."

The decadent weight she'd been basking under eased as he shifted to his elbows and peered down into her eyes. *Familiar eyes.*

Oh, God.

"It's fun to play and all, but I didn't want you to wonder or worry about who you were with. My name's Garrett."

"Garrett…Carter?" Her throat closed over the name, fighting what she knew deep in the pit of her stomach to be true.

His muscles tensed. "You know me?"

Oh, yeah. She knew him. And her face must have said as much because Garrett flinched, looking pained and then…resigned. Moving to a chair in the corner, he grabbed the light quilt from the back and tossed it to her.

Shoving one leg into his jeans, and then the other, he pulled them over his hips before he turned back. "I don't know what you heard, but this—tonight, Nichole—it's not—"

He stood immobile, his gaze searing over her skin, her hair—sweeping across her bedroom until it settled at the ladder-style bookshelf at the opposite side of the room. His body seemed to lock tight. She knew what he'd see there. The photo Maeve had given her for Christmas last year. The one where their grinning faces filled the frame.

He took a halting step forward, his features hardening.

His eyes slammed shut. "Nichole?"

Pulling the quilt around her breasts, she tried to ignore the sensitivity of her nipples and the knowledge *Garrett* had made them that way. With his mouth. His teeth. Tongue—

"*Nikki Daniels?*"

Garrett Carter. Maeve's brother. *The Panty Whisperer.*

Yeah, she couldn't quite believe it either.

Stalking across the room as he raked his fingers through his hair, Garrett—because, as clumsy as it felt tumbling around her thoughts, that's what his name was—looked as dismayed as she felt. One thing was certain. She didn't have to worry about the night turning into anything more complicated than—well, *this*.

Granted, *this* was messy. But the makings of some emotional train wreck it wasn't.

Maeve would laugh about this. Nichole knew she would. She had to.

There wasn't any risk to their relationship—not over one innocuous little slip she hadn't seen coming.

"What is that?" demanded the voice that had been growling her name in her ear mere minutes before.

Her head snapped up and then followed Garrett's pointed gaze back to her hand and the slim rectangle of technology she'd unconsciously reached for. "My phone."

Her lifeline to sorting out the mess in her head. To Maeve reassuring her their friendship was as strong as ever. There wouldn't be any awkwardness. Not this time. Not like with—

"No kidding. A phone, Nikki?"

Jerked back from the brink of one of the worst memories of her life, Nichole refocused on the man glowering down at her.

Her brow pushed up a degree. So now she was *Nikki*? Like *Garrett* thought he knew her or something? But before she could call him on his presumption he was back at her.

"What are you doing with it?"

Nothing yet. But the intent was obvious. Even if it had taken a moment for her head to catch up to her thumbs. "Texting Maeve."

He'd crossed to the bed in two strides.

"Like hell you are." Paling, he grabbed her hand and turned it over in his. "If you snapped a picture of me on this thing, so help me—"

"What? Are you insane? You think I took photos of you when you were...were...doing *that*?"

Arms folded over his chest, Garrett pulled back. "No. I hadn't actually thought—" Another, deeper growl. "But you tried to take a picture of me at the party."

"And you said no, so I didn't. Though in retrospect I'm fairly certain both of us would have preferred I had."

What Garrett had given her was beyond anything she could have imagined. But regardless of how good it had felt—how much she might have needed it—nothing was worth risking her relationship with Maeve.

Brows drawn, he asked, "You think Maeve would have warned you off me?"

Seriously? "Don't you?"

Granted it would have been for reasons different than Nichole's, but, yes, she was fairly certain Maeve would have wanted her to know who she was about to take a dip with.

One dark brow cocked in amusement. "I think she'd have been laughing too hard to hit 'send.' But for you, she'd have tried."

Nichole felt her lips twitching at the thought, along with relief flooding through her at hearing Garrett too believed Maeve would have a good sense of humor about this. "You could be right."

Garrett sat at the foot of the bed—not close enough to touch, but not a total snub either. Just maintaining the distance between them.

Snaking a leg out from beneath the blanket's overlap, she stretched, trying to reach the panties lying three feet from the bed without actually leaving it.

There was something significantly different about

being naked in front of Garrett now that she knew who he was. What he was.

At risk of severe cramp, she strained further, extending her leg until finally she was able to snare the little heap of lace-edged cotton with her toes. Only just as she had them Garrett turned, one arm braced on the bed, muscles bunched thick from the weight of his torso, and cocked a curious brow at her. "What are you doing?"

"Panties."

His brow drew down as his gaze flickered over the length of her barely concealed form, making her pull and pluck at the corners of the blanket to try and hide further beneath it.

"You really didn't know who I was?" he asked, pushing to his feet.

"I would have run the other way. No offense," she offered belatedly, wondering whether it was possible *not* to take offense.

But apparently he hadn't. "No, that's good."

"Why?"

"I just didn't like the idea of what happened tonight being some kind of conquest thing."

She sat up straighter. "This from The Panty Whisperer?"

Garrett froze where he was, jeans pulled over his hips but the fly left open. Bare feet, bare chest, the short dark waves of his hair a tousled mess... It would have been a calendar-hot snapshot in time if not for the hard set of his jaw and narrowed eyes. "You did *not* just call me that."

"Well, I mean..."

He paced the room and back. Coming to stop in front of her.

"What?" he demanded, thumbs hooked into the front pockets of his jeans—a position that pushed them down just that extra inch in front, showing off a nearly scandalous stretch of skin. "You're not suggesting I 'whispered' *you* out of anything?"

With a noncommittal wave she tried to bat away the question. In three years she hadn't even been tempted by another man. And in less than one night she'd fallen flat on her back and practically begged him to follow her down. If that wasn't some kind of freakish sexual panty magic she didn't know what was.

FIVE

—

Fighting the string of obscenities rioting on the tip of his tongue, Garrett ground his molars together and pinched the bridge of his nose.

It didn't get worse than this.

Well, that wasn't true. It did get worse. It *had* been worse. Back when he'd been eighteen and his older sister's friends had been trying to hook up with him intentionally. That had been way worse.

This, at least, was an accident.

Nikki. Hell, no wonder he'd had that bizarre sense of connection. He'd been listening to Maeve talk about her for years. He knew she'd grown up in Milwaukee, worked insane hours as an accountant at some big downtown firm, liked action movies over chick-flicks, read everything from sci-fi to biographies and that her favorite snack was peanut butter cups and corn chips. She sang along to the radio, badly, when she thought no one was listening and she didn't date—ever.

So what the hell was she doing tumbling into bed with him? Bringing some *stranger* into her home?

Garrett's stomach dropped as his feet stilled on the carpet.

It was all that talk about appreciating the simple stuff.

Aw, hell. Maybe he *had* "whispered" her.

"Um...Garrett?"

The muscles along his spine tightened as he turned to look back and found her clutching that damn phone to her chest like some kind of security blanket.

"Look, I'm sorry, but I'm not going to lie to Maeve about this."

She thought he was worried about Maeve finding out? Not even close.

"If she teases you, you'll just have to man up and take it."

Man up? He laughed out loud. Nikki was definitely one of his sister's friends, because no one else on the planet would have the gall to talk to him like that.

"I'm not worried about a little teasing." Though he knew full well there wouldn't be anything *little* about it. The teasing would be merciless, carried out by a seasoned professional he'd trained himself. But teasing he could take. It was part of the deal. *You dish it, you better be able to take it.*

"So what's the problem, then?" she asked, working the thin cover until it was wrapped around her, pulled up tight to her neck.

And that was the first thing. The sight of a woman

who had been so completely open to him not twenty minutes ago—bare and beautiful and unselfconscious as she panted for more, urged him on with the dig of her heels at his back and begged him not to stop. That woman—his little sister's best friend—who hadn't had sex in three years and for some insane reason had brought *him* back to her bed—was hiding awkwardly behind a blanket. That was the problem. He hated it.

Clearing his throat, he answered, "You deserve better."

The second thing. Maybe a part of him was disappointed. Felt short-changed.

He'd thought for a moment they could have *something*. Obviously he wasn't after a deep commitment or extended obligation. He needed another responsibility like he needed a hole in his head. But something light. Fun.

She'd seemed really fun. And intelligent. And just... *easy* in a way that had nothing to do with the kind of women he'd been scratching his itch with the past fifteen years. The kind who knew the score and weren't after anything more than he was. A few hours. Once in a while.

Nichole had made him think about things like movies and conversation and walks and all the stuff an average joe had tried on for size back in high school or college. Not that he'd tell her all that. She didn't need to know. Probably wouldn't believe him anyway, considering how easily that Panty Whisperer business had rolled off her tongue.

Damn, he could only imagine all the preconceived notions she must have about him. And the truth of it was, letting her hold on to them would serve his purpose better than any of the clarifications he could make. Because she was Maeve's best friend. Which meant all the concerns he'd never had with other women were suddenly there, front and center.

He couldn't attempt something casual with her because he'd worry about the implications his relationship *with her* would have on the one *she had with Maeve*. On *his* relationship with Maeve. And even though he was looking for more than some single night score, the relationship he was ready for was about taking in the occasional sunset...not riding off into one. It was about enjoying some pleasurable company for a while...not forever.

It was about *dating*. Casually—his eyes cut back to Nichole—but exclusively.

"Look, Nikki, you're an amazing girl, but I don't date my sisters' friends. It's a rule I've got."

Her expression cleared and she was leaning toward him then, the blanket draping more provocatively than she could have realized, based on the shy way she'd been covering up just moments before. He tried not to let his eye linger on the seductive gaps and tantalizing glimpses of the flesh he'd had full access to and could still feel beneath his fingers and lips, but were now completely off-limits. Round. Soft. Succulent. The kind of tempting swells that begged to be nipped and nibbled. Licked and suckled.

The sound of a throat clearing in a pointed, eyes-up-here-mister kind of way had Garrett yanked out of that land of forbidden territory and rubbing a hand along the tightening muscles of his neck.

"Okay, I know you're freaking out a little right now."

The hand stilled as he arched a brow at the woman who'd just uttered the impossible. "Excuse me?"

Those bare shoulders were pulled up into a delicate shrug as she waved a hand around in his direction. "But you honestly don't need to be. I didn't have any misconceptions about what was happening tonight. Where it could go or what it could mean. *Really.*"

Uh-huh. "You don't need to pretend with me, Nikki. I think we both know—"

"No, Garrett. I don't know what you *think* you know about me. But—"

"I know it's been three years. And before that dry spell you'd gone out with precisely two guys. Both of whom you ended up engaged to. So I'd say, yeah, you probably were serious." Too serious for a guy like him.

"So, I'm going to pretend it doesn't creep me out that you know that. And I'll wait until you leave to have my discussion with your sister about privacy, trust and boundaries—"

Oh, man. This was going downhill fast. Holding out a staying hand, he tried not to get caught up in all the ways the bit of red rushing to the skin at Nichole's neck and shoulders was different than what he'd sampled earlier.

"What?" she snapped.

"Don't get pissed at Maeve about this." And already with the complications a simple exchange of names might have avoided. "Please. She was just giving me some reassurance about the crowd she hung around with. Making sure I knew you weren't trouble. That you were...you know...into commitment...a 'nice girl.'" There was something about the slow upward push of her brows that warned of danger, had him backtracking as he tried another tack. "Not that I don't think you're nice now."

"You should probably just stop, Garrett."

Yeah, he probably should. Get out of there and get started on figuring out what it was going to take to appease his little sister when she found out he'd gotten her into hot water with her closest girlfriend. Only the way things were right now—hell, less than a single night and already he felt the press of new responsibility settling on his shoulders—he needed to know she was okay.

She'd trusted him. Let him into her bed. "Nikki—"

"Here's the thing." Shaking her head, Nichole tucked a wild curl neatly behind her ear. "Tonight was an accident. An error in judgment on both our parts. So why don't we both agree to put it behind us? I mean, it's not like we've been tripping over each other these last few years. I'm guessing it's a pretty safe bet our paths won't cross again anytime soon. And, believe me, I'm okay with that. This wasn't supposed to be more than a single night anyway."

He blinked. No way. She was just being tough to protect her pride.

Except those almond eyes were steady, clear as they held his. And wasn't that an ironic twist? The first woman he'd pursued with the intent of having something "more" didn't see him as anything more than the kind of one-night stand he'd been ready to leave behind.

It shouldn't have rubbed—but, *man*.

Shaking it off, because he knew it was for the best, Garrett nodded his acceptance. Walked back to the bed and, catching the soft line of her jaw in his palm, tipped her face to drop a kiss at her temple. "I'm sorry about this, Nikki."

She blinked at him, the corner of her mouth tipping the barest amount. "Don't be. I'm not."

Two hours later and Nichole had given up on the idea of sleep altogether. And if ever there was a time for a BFF to step up it was after she'd been busted selling out the details of her friend's nonexistent sex-life to The Panty Whisperer. Which was why Nichole was parked in front of her laptop, staring down the video feed as—across the country—Maeve paced in a knee length T-shirt in front of her own laptop.

"It's not like I was detailing the chronicles of your personal *Red Shoe Diaries* on Twitter, for God's sake."

Nichole balled her hands on her hips, glaring through cyberspace as she waited Maeve out.

It didn't take long before her friend gave under the

pressure, her entire form signaling defeat as the arms crossed defiantly over her chest went spaghetti-loose along with the rest of her body and she spilled into the couch behind her. "Okay, I'm sorry! I shouldn't have told anyone about your personal business and I don't even know why exactly I did—except Garrett isn't like a real person. He's just got this knack for extracting information from people. He's patient. Unrelenting. And when he wants to know something... nothing gets in his way."

This she'd heard before. But it didn't change one simple fact. "My sexual experience is none of his business."

None.

God, the way he'd looked at her so apologetically as he'd nailed her with the "commitment" tag and "nice girl" nonsense. This guy she'd brought home without even knowing his name had wrapped her up in all the labels she'd spent three years trying to shed. She wasn't looking to get married. Didn't want—*anything*. Especially not from him, and so it didn't matter what he thought.

With that reminder, Nichole blew out a stiff breath.

Sliding the arm flung across her eyes up to her brow, Maeve frowned at her. "I know. I know. And I really am sorry. But now that you've met him, how can you even wonder about his ability to get what he wants?"

Nichole shook her head. "The guy lives in town. If he's so worried about your lifestyle why doesn't he meet your friends?"

Maeve stared up at the ceiling. "When it comes to my dates, given the opportunity, you better believe he's all over them. But girlfriends not so much. You know that saying about having to beat women off with a stick? That's what it was like for him with Bethany's, Carla's and Erin's friends. Mine to a lesser extent. But he avoids our girlfriends pretty much like the plague. Besides, the last few years he's been so tied up with building the company and working to get his degree there hasn't been a whole lot of time for anything else. I barely see him."

Nichole blinked as another piece of the puzzle fell into place. She'd forgotten about the school thing. A detail Maeve had shared with her. Garrett had put all of his sisters through school and only started himself when everyone else had been paid for and finished.

"So that's what he meant by saying he was trying to get back to living a little."

Maeve, casting all dramatics aside, sat upright, leaning forward. "Really? What else did he say?"

Suddenly Nichole felt unsure about the lines in this family dynamic she'd somehow gotten tangled in. Rather than try to sort them out, she opted to put the conversation back on track. "Okay, I know you would never be careless with my privacy or indifferent to my feelings—it just took me by surprise." Like so many things that evening. "But from now on can we agree—?"

Maeve waved her off with a shake of her head. "I

swear. Never again. Not another word about your sexual experience to him."

Nichole arched a brow. "How about you just leave me out of the conversation completely?"

Maeve's mouth squinched up and she cocked her head. "Yeah, that's probably not entirely realistic. This is Garrett we're talking about. And now that you're on his radar I imagine he's going to feel a little protective of you. Which means I'm probably going to be answering some questions from time to time."

Nichole's mouth popped open, but Maeve just shrugged. "He kind of can't help himself. So...welcome to my world!"

"Maeve!"

Her friend sprang up from her slump at the couch and hustled right up in front of her laptop, resting her chin in the vee of her palms. "So now that we're back to being besties again...on a scale of skim milk to heavy whipping cream...."

Garrett pried one eyelid open, scowling hard as the screeching of a tiny banshee emanating from down the hall reached his ears.

"I know you're there, Garrett Carter. You pick up this phone right now or so help me...."

So help her, what? She was going to fly home and jab her little finger at his chest? Scowl up at him with those eyes that said he'd betrayed her in the most fundamental way and she was both hurt and disappointed?

Garrett's other eye was open and his feet were swinging over the side of the bed in a second flat. Reaching for the extension at his nightstand with one hand, he rubbed at his morning stubble with the other.

"A little early, isn't it, Maeve?"

"You're alone?"

He blew his breath out with a good deal of his patience. "It's only been..." squinting at the clock, he noted it was just after five "...a few hours since I left her apartment. Do you really think I'd stop and pick up someone else on the way back?"

The answering silence said she wouldn't put it past him.

"Geez, yes, I'm alone. And, for what it's worth, I had no idea who she was."

A little hiss sounded through the line. "Yeah, but everyone else did. What were you even doing at Sam's party?"

"It was a party for his brother. You know Jesse? My oldest friend? Artist? Touring for the past two years? Any of this ringing a bell? So, Nikki's close with Sam?"

"We're out with him, like, once a week at least. He's part of the core crowd."

Garrett's brows dropped down, the fog of sleep clearing faster now. "Wait. He hangs out with that old crowd from my class—"

"Give me a break, Garrett. I see Sam and the guys all the time. These days they're more my friends than yours."

What the—?

"I'm not surprised you don't know. Aside from the fact you've been AWOL for the last few years, doing your twenty-two-hours-a-day summa-cum-look-at-Superman-earning-top-honors-while-running-his-company thing, you've got a reputation as kind of a psycho when it comes to your sisters. I wasn't about to tell you, and it doesn't surprise me no one else had the guts to do it either."

This time the deafening silence was booming out of his corner as he let that little gem sink in.

Maeve.

Hanging out with *his* friends.

A pack of low-life scum who thought the nickname Panty Whisperer bad-ass enough to *ooh* and *aah* at its inception, giving high-fives and back-slaps as though going home with whomever it had been back then hadn't simply been some callow escape, but a conquest worth celebration.

They'd been hanging out with his little sister.

And lying to him about it.

"Oh, wait. Before you flip. I'm not talking about Joey and those guys. Mostly Sam. Once in a while Rafe and Mitch show up. And, to be clear, I don't date any of them. Ever."

A relieved breath hissed through his teeth and a few seconds later his jaw unlocked too.

"Helloo? Earth to Panty Whisperer, betrayer of sisters' trust everywhere."

Wow. Little Maeve with the one-two punch. The girl

knew how to drop a bomb and then turn the tables in a heartbeat. God help the guy who landed *her*.

"Maeve, just give me a minute to catch up. To wake up, okay?"

He could hear her tongue clucking through the line. Could practically see that impatient posture and pouty scowl. The same one she'd been pulling since she was six years old. Of course back then it wouldn't have been directed at him. Back then he'd been her hero. The one to intervene on her behalf with older sisters who didn't want clumsy hands breaking their stuff.

"Ready yet?"

"Yeah, why not? Go ahead and give it to me." He pushed up from the bed, figuring there wouldn't be any getting back to it after this, and headed in search of sustenance of the coffee-and-cookies variety.

"I can't believe you told Nikki you knew how long it had been since she had sex. I can't *believe*, after you figured out who she was, you would be so thoughtless as to violate my trust like that. And you didn't just stop at...."

Pushing the start button on the coffeepot, he grunted his acknowledgment of wrongdoing, knowing it would be a move just short of suicide to interrupt the rant in progress for the petty satisfaction of pointing out that *she'd* broken Nichole's trust first.

Garrett was halfway through his first cup of coffee when the quiet from the other end of the line hit a point where it was clear this wasn't just Maeve taking a breath, but she was waiting for a response.

Setting the mug aside, Garrett rubbed a palm over the smooth finish of his kitchen table. "So, aside from being pissed you'd told me about her dating history, did she sound okay?"

There was another silence from across the miles, though this one Garrett wasn't quite sure how to read.

Then, "She was fine. Why wouldn't she be?"

"You know. Because she's a commitment girl." He still didn't know how they'd gotten their lines crossed so badly. In all these years he'd never made such a mess—

"Oh, that. Yeah. Get over yourself, Garrett. She wasn't looking for serious with you. Which I'm pretty sure she actually told you already."

Yeah, she had. But maybe he just hadn't liked the sound of it. Or maybe he hadn't wanted to believe it was true because for some reason he didn't like the idea of it in the context of her...with him.

"Okay, I can practically hear you worrying over there. But you're going to have to take my word for it. Nikki is fine. This was exactly what she needed. Except the part about it being *you* and all."

Thank you, Maeve.

"She wanted to prove to herself she could have a little fun without it having to turn into some white-dress event. And she did. So no biggie." Maeve let out a giggle in the background. "Though next time I'm guessing she'll get the guy's name first."

Next time.

Garrett closed his eyes against the words. Figured

out it only facilitated the mental peep show—Nichole leaning back on her bed with those big brown eyes peering up at...*not him*. Hell.

Walking over to the counter, he refilled his mug and threw half of it back at once. Time to wake up and get on with the new day.

"Yeah. Hopefully."

SIX

—

Nichole sank the six and watched the cue ball come to rest neatly behind the four. Nice.

Across the felt landscape Maeve tapped her foot impatiently against the leg of her stool, watching as Nichole adjusted her stance and lined up her shot.

"Wow, your form's really improved."

Nichole paused, glanced up. "Huh?"

"No, really." All nonchalance, Maeve waved toward the pool cue, the twitch at the corner of her mouth a warning of what was to come.

Hard to believe it had only been a week with the amount of ribbing she'd taken. But there it was. A week since she'd had the hot press of Garrett's mouth against hers, the weight of his body—

"You've got a firm grasp on that *butt*...while the *shaft* just glides through your fingers. I don't know... it's almost like you've had some practice with the *wood* lately."

Mouth hanging open, Nichole fought the slow burn

spreading across her cheeks and neck...and lost. "Seriously?"

Maeve smirked. "Ohh, shoot! Your alignment just went to hell."

"You wish."

Leaning over the table she straightened out the shot, drew back, focused—

"Gentle with the tip."

—and scratched. "Maeve!"

Her friend looked less than chagrined. "What? This is pool. I was working the lingo. Whatever your depraved mind does with it is on you." Jumping from the stool, she winked. "Plus, I really want to win!"

Nichole waited until Maeve was all lined up before settling a hip at the side of the table. "You know, Maeve, there's more to the game than your stroke. *The stick you choose*, for example."

An expression of horror crept over Maeve's face. "You wouldn't."

No, she wouldn't.

Well, maybe just a little. "I recently had my hands on a nice hard *wood*. I think I'll tell you about it. In detail. Let's start with—"

"Enough!" Maeve's frantic squeak was punctuated by the one-two thud of the eight and the cue sinking in short order. "You win! Oh, my God, I feel dirty."

Nichole tossed her hair over her shoulder, reveling in the victory. "As you should, cheater."

"Yeah, yeah," Maeve grumbled, too competitive to let any loss go without at least a brief sulk and most likely one more go at retaliation. Only she seemed to shake it off in a blink, her smile returning to full blast. "So, what do you want from the bar?"

"Whatever. You pick."

Maeve leaned in and craned her neck in an exaggerated manner. "Garrett? You want something too?"

Nichole froze in her spot as the skin across her back began to tingle and burn.

"Hey, Nikki, maybe Garrett would like to hear what you thought about that stick you were using? How much you liked the feel of that hard wood and all? Heck, maybe he could even help you perfect your hold!" And with that she darted off for the bar.

He wasn't there. He couldn't be.

And yet even as she turned she knew.

Her gaze started at the floor and the size-twelve boots planted in a wide stance less than a handful of feet away, crawled up the saddle-brown twill of cargo-style pants and followed the gray long-sleeve tee stretched to perfection over his torso before making the unsettling jump to firm lips slanted in an off-kilter smile and the single raised brow demanding clarification.

"Maeve just being Maeve?" he asked, and the breath Nichole hadn't realized she'd been holding rushed out in relief.

No lie necessary. "Exactly."

Only those too intense blue eyes narrowed the slightest bit. "So the *wood* you guys were talking about was really...wood?"

She hadn't believed it was possible to choke on words that weren't her own, but there she was, sputtering as though she'd swallowed a string of oversized letters cut from rough stone. They blocked the pathway from her lungs to her mouth, making the intake of breath an impossible thing.

Lie. Simple. Just lie now and everything would be fine.

Except she could already feel his gaze following the hot path of her heated skin over her cheeks, down her neck...lower.

Clearing her throat, she dug in the front pocket of her jeans, pulling out a couple of quarters. "We were talking about pool. Sticks. Cues."

The corner of his mouth twitched and his eyes flashed back to hers. "Shafts and butts?"

"Technical terms."

Garrett stepped closer, resting his hand at her waist as he bowed his head toward her ear, close enough so she could smell the clean masculine scent of him. Soap and skin and the barest hint of lingering sawdust. Close enough so fingers of warmth from his body could reach out and touch hers. Close enough to send her senses reeling as his breath washed over her ear, carrying his gruff, taunting words. "Yeah? Why don't you tell me about it?"

Nichole's eyes flew wide with her mouth. "No— nothing," she managed, stumbling back only to be steadied by Garrett's strong hand.

"Liar, liar, pants on fire," he laughed in challenge. Then, with a conspiratorial wink, added, "Red."

And with a word she was back to that night.

To the flirtation, the slow pulling need, the fast-rising hunger. Dim hallways and dark shadows. His mouth, his hands, his body...his name.

Garrett.

Her eyes pinched shut as she cleared her mind and drew a cleansing breath. "What are you doing here?"

"Jesse." He nodded toward the table across the bar where she and Maeve had been sitting with the guys before starting their game of pool. "I didn't expect to see you."

And, though he hadn't tried to avoid her, it was pretty clear if he had known, he wouldn't have come. She got it. That was how one-nighters went. *One night.*

"I didn't know you were coming either." If she had she might have glanced at her hair before she left home. Gone for the cherry ChapStick instead of the original. She might have worn a skirt.

And not with the expectation that those big hands would find their way under it. No!

She cleared her head with a stern shake.

"It was a last-minute thing. Deciding to come out. But..." His jaw cocked to one side as his gaze slid over the second-floor bar before returning to search her eyes. "I don't have to stay if this is uncomfortable for you."

Nichole was already shaking her head when a tall glass of what was probably rum and Coke cut between them, followed by Maeve's disgusted voice. "Didn't I tell you to get over yourself? Nikki couldn't care less about you showing up here."

Not exactly true, but at least it was Maeve saying it instead of her. And, judging from the glint of amusement in Garrett's eyes, his little sister's biting words didn't faze him.

His focus shifted to Maeve. "How'd that job in Denver work out?"

"Same ol', same ol'." Maeve shrugged, snaking an arm around her brother's waist for a quick hug. "I'm scheduled to go back next week."

Nichole watched the two fall into the conversation she knew one side of by heart, and wondered how it was possible she hadn't recognized Garrett for who he was.

Only on some level she had. She'd seen his face at least a hundred times in photos in Maeve's old albums. And, though most of those pictures were of a kid rather than a man, some of them had been recent. Which had to be the reason for that sense of connection. The immediate *click*.

Watching them together now, though, there was one thing she couldn't miss. Being around Garrett wasn't going to be a problem in any sense. His focus on Maeve was utterly complete.

There wasn't any lingering tension—at least not from his side. He'd showed up, said hello when he saw her, been friendly and then moved on as though nothing had happened between them at all.

Maeve had been right about her brother being the expert in keeping relationships simple. And lucky Nichole to have the Panty Whisperer for her mentor.

Garrett stood with his back to the bar, his eyes focused on the pool table across the room where Nichole was lining up her shot, his tongue lodged somewhere halfway down his throat.

She moved from one spot to another, bending at the waist, bracing her weight with a hand on the table, widening her stance until—

Until every damn guy in the bar was leering as she took her shot. Just like him. The only thing setting him apart from the rest of the hounds panting after her was *he* knew just exactly what he was missing. He knew what it felt like to kneel between those legs. He knew what it felt like to spread his palm over the flat of her belly. To run his tongue the length of her.

Which meant, right then, he envied them. At least they could tell themselves it probably wouldn't be as good as their imagination was making it.

Nichole let out a whoop, high-fiving Maeve as two guys he didn't know took losing with dopey grins and an offer of more drinks.

Garrett's eyes narrowed as he started sizing them up. They looked harmless, but guys put on a lot of façades.

His gaze shot over to his sister, who seemed to be handling the attention fine, passing on the drinks— good girl—and whatever else the guys were offering.

Same as Nichole. Only there was something different about the way the two women handled it. Maeve leaned into the conversation, taking the flattery with grace even as she rejected it, while Nichole simply didn't seem to register it at all. She was smiling freely at the guys, but without any kind of sexual recognition whatsoever.

Even when one of the guys reached for her hand, trying to angle in for some eye contact, she just wrapped her free hand around his fingers and basically handed them back to him...with a smile.

She was *friendly*.

Like he'd never seen "friendly" done before. Some girls played at it. Used it like a kind of game of push-and-pull. But Nichole...she was completely open and available only in one clearly identifiable way that said "not a chance" without ever having to say it at all.

"What's up, man?"

Garrett shot a look over his shoulder to where Jesse was moving in beside him, his brother Sam a step behind.

"Just wondering how in the hell I ever got past that," he answered with a nod in Nichole's direction.

Jesse's hands came up with the corners of his mouth. "Don't look at me. I thought about asking her out back before I left, but she 'friended' me so fast there was no point in even trying."

Jesse was one of the few friends Garrett had maintained regular interaction with over the years. He'd been a mellow, genuine guy from as far back as Garrett could remember. And through those first years after losing his dad, when it had seemed like the world was going to collapse around his shoulders and there was no way he'd be able to *be everything* he needed to be for everyone who needed it, Jesse had unrelentingly been there for him, refusing to let Garrett be alone no matter that the life he'd been a part of—the one with sports and chicks and hanging out—was gone. He'd been the guy to get his twenty-four-year-old sister to babysit once a month so Garrett could go out for a couple hours. The one who hadn't crowed about cheap conquests. The one who'd understood. Maybe his artist's mentality gave him more insight than the other meatheads. Whatever. He was a good friend—one of the only ones he truly felt comfortable confiding in.

An hour later Garrett was having to put significantly more effort into not feeling like a stalker than he generally cared to. But, honest to God, he just couldn't keep his eyes from working their way back to that auburn tumble of hair and contagious laugh.

"She like this with everyone?" he asked Sam, watching as she yucked it up with yet another group of what he'd bet good money had been strangers until just that night. It seemed like she could talk to anyone about anything.

"What do you mean—friendly, easygoing?" Sam flagged the bartender for another round. Then, at Garrett's nod, he shrugged. "Pretty much. But she can take care of herself. With one recent exception, nobody gets past her 'friend' zone. Some jack-off burned her pretty bad a few years ago and she's been avoiding the flames ever since. So you don't really need to worry about looking out for her. Aside from doing a damn good job of it herself, she's got a lot of people who care about how she gets treated."

There was an edge in those last words that had Garrett's head cranking around to where Sam was watching him, a matter-of-fact look in his eyes. "You talking about me?"

Jesse covered his mouth with his hand, but a low laugh escaped regardless.

There was no way Jesse's little brother was warning *him* off of Nichole? But, sure enough, he was.

"Relax, man. I'm not going anywhere near her."

"You've already been near her. And the way you've been watching her all night...."

Garrett was about to tell Sam he was nuts when that same sort of gravitational pull had him turning around again...and locking eyes with Nichole. Who'd been watching him.

Her lips parted, and from across the room he could actually feel the catch of *her* breath in *his* chest.

And then there it was—that blaze of heat working up her neck and cheeks. The one that made him wonder if he would feel the change it brought against his lips if they were positioned in just the right spot.

The corner of his mouth edged up as he tapped his cheek, mouthing the word *red* to the woman he was suddenly alone with across the expanse of this crowded bar.

Her answering smile was too many kinds of different to count from what she'd been giving to every other guy there tonight, and it hit him like a pile-driver to the gut, effectively knocking the wind out of him as he turned back to his closest friend and shook his head in genuine bewilderment.

Jesse let out a low chuckle. "I'm starting to wonder if the real question isn't how you got past her, but how *she* got past *you*."

SEVEN

"You again?" Nichole cocked a brow at Garrett as he slid into an empty seat across the narrow table running the length of the trendy downtown gastropub. Not that she was surprised. After three weeks of bumping into the guy most every time she went out, these rendezvous were becoming the rule rather than the exception.

At first they'd both been surprised. Accepting. Maybe even amused.

When it had become obvious that the crossing of their paths wasn't simply a fluke but a consequence of the overlap of their friends, they'd found a few minutes to talk away from everyone else, both wanting to ensure the other was comfortable.

And they were. Mostly.

The conversation always came easily. Naturally. So much so that by the end of an evening more often than not she and Garrett would discover they'd been so caught up in their own interaction they'd lost the rest of the group along the way. Which was when things became the littlest bit less comfortable.

The laughter would die down between them, the break between one topic and the next filling with an awareness of the things they didn't want. They'd look around for another conversation to dive into, but they'd be alone. Which would lead to the moment when her focus would drop to his mouth, the open collar of his shirt, a button or two even lower...

And then she'd realize how late it was. Or he'd remember the early call he had to get up for. Or they'd both catch sight of someone and quickly return to the group, going on as they had before, figuring it would get easier along the way.

Eventually.

Only as Garrett's long legs brushed hers beneath the polished benchtop, and her breath sucked in with the unwilling image of their legs caught together in a tangle of heat and skin, she realized *eventually* couldn't happen soon enough.

"Red," came the gruff observation from across the table. Quiet enough the rest of the group, chatting in their usual animated fashion, didn't seem to catch it.

But if anyone had bothered to look up as she had, no one would have missed the heat in Garrett's eyes.

"It'll go away," she murmured, flipping her menu open in the hopes of shielding herself to some degree.

Only then the contact that had been inadvertent just the moment before was back. This time blatant and intentional. The press of his leg along hers, holding until she met his eyes.

"I'm starting to wonder."

Garrett glared into the men's room mirror after trying to stop the low simmer running through his veins with a cold splash of water. It wasn't working.

So much for thinking this coffee shop concert would keep him out of trouble just because they wouldn't be able to talk. He'd seen her. Seen when her eyes met his. And he didn't need words because already he knew too much about her. And every damn time he went out...whether Nichole was actually there are or not... he found out more.

And, God help him, he liked it all.

She was cool and funny and clever and thoughtful and generous and loyal...and, *damn it*, he knew just exactly how good she tasted on his tongue.

And he couldn't have her. Because he didn't want her. And she didn't want him.

They'd talked about it. More than once. Probably more than they needed to. Except for some reason it was one of those topics that seemed to require excessive amounts of reinforcement. He was starting to think maybe this girly splash of cold water wasn't the way to go. He needed the reason hammered into his head.

Handy that he owned his own construction company. He ought to be able to find someone to do it for him.

With a hard shake of his head, he stalked out of the men's room into the back hallway and came up short at the sight of Nichole at the far end.

This was the problem. The pull. With words or without, it was like there was some kind of force drawing them together...and it wouldn't stop until they were as close as two bodies could be.

Yeah.

Echoes of the classical guitar they'd come to the coffee house to hear filled the otherwise deserted space as he closed the distance between them. Watched with the kind of satisfaction that should have made him ashamed as Nichole's eyes went wide with understanding and she looked for a means of escape. Only in the end they both knew she didn't want to get away any more than he wanted her to.

And then he had her. He hooked a finger through the belt loop of her jeans, giving himself mad props for refraining from sliding that finger between the denim and the bare skin of her belly the way he wanted to.

Tugging gently, he pulled her down the hall, away from where the intimate concert was being held toward a flight of stairs that led to a second floor.

"What's up there?" Nichole asked, craning a bit to try and see around the bend as Garrett led the way.

"No idea. But we need to talk."

A quick shake of her head. "I just came to say goodbye. I've— I think— I need to take off early tonight."

Because the tension between them was growing

thicker with every encounter. Every exchange. Every accidental or even not so accidental brush.

And she'd wised up.

Only too late.

"You can't just—just corral me like this, Garrett," she laughed nervously, working her way up the steps backward even when she had to know the only escape was from the other direction.

Of course he could. And unless she actually used the magic word *no*, he would. "That first night, Nichole... why did you let me take you home?"

Nichole stopped, caught in the dark pull of eyes she never should have looked into.

They'd talked about this. To a degree. But neither of them had been able to move past it. Get free of what had happened and the lingering connection that kept pulling them back to it.

"Because when I met you it was the first time in as long as I could remember I wanted more than friendship." Another backward step and she nearly tripped on the stair. But Garrett was there, his hand at her elbow, steadying her even as he crowded her back.

What was he doing? Being this close, asking her about that night...it was a mistake. They couldn't go on like this. At first it had been all fun and games. The lingering tension and chemistry between them almost a joke. A dirty secret they shared. Something amusing. A challenge to overcome.

But as the weeks moved past, as the tension and

temptations grew, having to say no to something she wanted with more urgency every time they met had ceased being funny.

Nichole *wanted* this man.

So much more than she should.

"I brought you home with me because I thought it would be safe. There wouldn't be any risk of getting involved, of things getting too complicated, of me—" She swallowed, closed her eyes and forced herself to say the rest of it. "Of me getting ahead of myself. Because I didn't even know your name."

She'd been so wrong. Because now not only did she know just exactly who she'd been with and precisely how to find him...she had to see him all the time.

"So, about that...." His fingers curved around her waist, ending her retreat where she stood, balanced on the third stair from the top of the landing in a space she had no right occupying.

Garrett took the next step, closing the distance between them until his chest brushed against hers and their breath mingled warm and wet together.

Her lashes fluttered as better judgment warred against *want*. "What are you doing?"

"Reminiscing. It was very hot."

She shouldn't have liked the sound of that so much. Not when there was no place to go with it. But the part of her that had never been entirely confident in the sexual arena...the part that even after years remained just the littlest bit bruised over the way her last relationship had ended...*needed* to know. Needed to hear. "My not wanting to know your name was hot?"

"No, that was just kinky fun."

It was everything she could do not to purr.

Kinky...*her?*

Oh, that was a first. One she'd savor.

"What was hot..." his voice dropped lower as he leaned closer toward her ear "...were the soft, throaty little moans you made and the way you gave your whole body over to me when I pulled you close."

Her mouth went dry and even the nervous butterflies batting about her stomach stilled...waited. "You're whispering me again."

Those eyes.

"Maybe I am."

His mouth.

"I thought we were friends. I thought we agreed."

The *heat.*

He nodded. "We did."

"Then why?"

Her jeans were snug with the tightening of Garrett's fists at her sides, adding to the sensation of his touch, his hold, extending beyond just his fingers to everywhere the fabric touched her. Around her hips, her bottom, between her legs and down her thighs.

"The strings are already there, Nichole. The lines have already been crossed. And if you really want to know, I cross them more every damn time I look at you. I can't stop thinking about hearing you make those sounds again. Only this time I want to hear them when you're saying my name."

"*Garrett*—"

"Hell, *yes*."

And then the space between them that was all potential and unmet need and *why* and *why not* was gone. Replaced by contact. Hot and concentrated. The mind-blowing sensation of Garrett's chest moving up against her own as he took that final step. Hard-packed muscle and cotton created a teasing friction against her nipples that left her breathless, lips still parted on a broken gasp when his head bowed to hers.

"Just like that." His words were a kiss against her lips. The soft brush before the bruising crush. The taste that warned it would never be enough.

Garrett.

His mouth moved against hers like an unspoken demand, rubbing slowly, telling her what he wanted, what she wanted to give him. He parted her lips beneath the insistent pressure of his own, working back and forth without giving her the "more" she ached for, stroking her need until it surpassed his own and she was wordlessly begging: with her hands—one clutching and releasing and then clutching again at the fabric of his shirt, the other flexed against all that contained strength, riding the peaks and valleys of a musculature she'd only believed existed in the land of airbrush and fiction. Begging with her body—bowed forward in an arch that was needy and shameless; with the same throaty whimper that had brought them to this point in the first place. The one that apparently did the trick, because in the next second she had what she wanted—Garrett's tongue thrusting past her parted lips, rolling against her own, delivering a deeper, more potent version of the moan he'd been talking about in the process, ensuring they were in fact together in this desperation.

And that was the most intoxicating part of it all. They were *together*.

Another thrust and the hands gripping her hips tightened. And then she was sucking lightly over his tongue, gasping at the flick of it against her bottom lip, getting lost in all the places only this man had been able to take her—in the physical sensations unique to being with him, in the slide of his arms around her back so one hand came to rest across her bottom and thigh and the other wound into her hair and tightened there so she felt his hold against a thousand points of contact within her skin.

Oh, and she knew what he was going to do next—whimpered in anticipation of a repeat of the move that had haunted her nights so relentlessly.

Garrett's lips curled against her own. "Say it."

"Garrett."

The tension at her scalp tightened incrementally as he used her hair to guide her head back, extending her neck further, opening her mouth to him so the kiss that came next was one he took. One he controlled. One he gave. One that made her groan and melt beneath it.

Made her ache through every point of contact yet to be made.

The hand across her bottom pulled her closer. Held her firm against the straining ridge of his erection.

Another whimper. Another reckless pant of his name.

Another thrust of his tongue into her waiting mouth.

All that mattered was this. More. Easing the almost painful clench of need so deep inside her.

And then the hand in her hair slipped free. Her head came up and in a daze she met the blue flame of Garrett's eyes...tried to close the distance between them he had opened. She reached for his shoulder, his hair. Leaned in to his kiss, getting less than a taste before he broke away again.

Too much. She'd gone too far again. Gotten carried away—

Except he had her hand in his. The muscle in his jaw was jumping as he raked his other hand through the hair that was standing up in a guilty mess. "There's got to be a back way out of here. Let's go. I think I can make it to my car."

The haze of arousal cleared further and Nichole looked around, stunned to find herself in this state of reckless abandon in the back hall of a coffee house. Oh, God. *Mistake!*

"Garrett, I can't."

He nodded, shoved his hand through his hair again and then grabbed her hips and lifted her up against him in a move so swift and deft she had her legs wrapped around his waist before she'd even realized what was happening.

No, this she had to stop—and fast. Because Garrett was carrying her up the last stairs, groaning some kind of agreement that neither could he. And then her back was against the wall and his hips were rocking against the needy spot between her legs that made her stupid in ways she could never have imagined prior to meeting him.

"Garrett," she gasped when his mouth closed over her neck.

And that totally hadn't come out the way it had been supposed to. But before she could even think about where she'd gone wrong with that one single critical word, the sensual, disorienting fog was descending again. Rolling in thicker with each flick of his tongue, every rock of his hips and brush of his thumb against the straining peak of her nipple.

Because, yes, this guy was plenty strong enough to hold her against the wall with one hand. And, God, wasn't that the hottest thing? Next to all the other billion hot things about him. She was a little ashamed to admit his being so worked up enough to do her against the back wall of a public place was one of them.

But it had to stop.

She needed to check her libido and her ego and—

"Garrrrett..."

What...how...that was...would he do it again?

Then his mouth was back at her ear. His breath a hot

rush against the tender tissue. His low growl a rough stroke against all the places where she ached for him. "Are you wet, Nichole?"

She opened her mouth, trying to form words—only her mind had blanked of coherent thought. And apparently Garrett didn't need an answer anyway, because somewhere along the way he'd gotten her fly undone, loosened the denim enough to skim his hand down the back.

"Aww, baby, you're *so*—"

"Stop."

She didn't know where she'd found the resolve to say it, or how Garrett had even heard, the word was so small. So not at all what she wanted. But there it was. And he had heard, because that marauding hand of his was working a steady retreat back to her hip, where he continued to hold her against him.

So maybe unlocking her ankles from the small of his back and letting go of his shirt and hair should be her next step.

Reluctantly, she did so. And, sure enough, Garrett eased her down to her feet from there. Let his forehead rest against hers and, with a pained groan, refastened her jeans. Because he was just that kind of guy.

Which made her want him all the more.

And that was a problem. Because Nichole wasn't ready for this.

Thanks to her deadbeat dad's underwhelming commitment to fatherhood she'd always been skittish about getting involved. The two guys she'd risked her heart with in the past had been more about building relationships than scoring bases. She'd known them for years, trusted them and made plans with them. With Paul...they'd been so young. When he'd ended things, she'd understood and recovered with only a few scars. But with Joel she'd been so hurt. So humiliated by what had happened it had taken her three years to brave up enough to dip just her toe back in.

Okay, fine. She'd done the full-on skinny-dip. But still... What she'd done she'd done believing it would be a one-time isolated incident with a guy who wouldn't be around twenty-four-seven, tempting her to invest more of her heart than she should.

Garrett murmured, "Nichole, this thing between us isn't going away."

No, it wasn't. "I'm not sure we're giving it much of a chance to."

"Maybe not." Pulling back, Garrett looked around them, as if just realizing exactly where they were, and swore. "I'm sorry about this. I don't know what I was—"

"Yeah, neither do I." With a quiet laugh, Nichole added, "You are *really* going to get the wrong idea about what kind of girl I am."

Garrett caught her chin with his finger and brought her gaze to his. "No, I won't."

Then, leading her down the flight, he stopped at the bottom stair and pulled her down to sit beside him. The guitarist had moved on to a new piece— something slow and soulful. Each pluck of the strings seemed weighted with a melancholy that resonated inside her.

Forearms resting over his widespread knees, Garrett scrubbed a palm over his face. "I know I'm the one who said this wouldn't work. That I didn't want it. But it sort of feels like we already have it, whether we meant to or not... Nichole, I can handle the part about Maeve."

"But I'm not sure I can." Maeve was her best friend. Her rock. The person she couldn't live without. The person she'd need to turn to if her heart ever got trampled again. "Let's just say you aren't the only one with a protective streak when it comes to your family."

Garrett's brows shot skyward, as though the thought had never occurred to him. "Are you worried you're going to break my heart and Maeve's going to hold it against you?"

"Well, no." While something told her Garrett's heart was immune to breaking, there were no guarantees when it came to hard feelings. "But she didn't take too kindly to an off-the-cuff remark I made last month. And that was before I'd actually even met you."

His expression closed down as he asked, "What kind of remark?"

Why had she brought it up? She didn't want to tell him what she'd said. Didn't want to risk his feelings or insult him. But he was staring at her, waiting. "Something about antibiotics. It was stupid and totally off-base and I apologize."

A nod. "The Panty Whisperer garbage. I get it. I've earned it."

Something about those last words and the weary resignation in them cut at her.

"Garrett, I didn't know anything about you. But I do now—"

At that, his mouth curved into a wry smile. "Yeah, and I'm betting what just happened at the top of these stairs pretty well backs up every rumor you've ever heard."

It might have if this connection she'd somehow formed with Garrett hadn't given her a deeper insight into who he was. Into what he valued. But he seemed as genuinely undone by the attraction between them as she was. Fighting it and trying to push it aside so they could enjoy a friendship regardless.

She didn't want her careless words to hurt him or undermine all there was to respect.

If ever she needed a lifeline it was now. She wanted Maeve to tell her what to say. Although now that she thought about it...

"I do have to admit I'm pretty impressed. I always sort of assumed the rumors were exaggerated. But, *damn*, Garrett."

He was a Carter, after all. And teasing was their foremost means of affection.

His sudden stunned bark of laughter was everything she'd wanted to hear. And then he leaned back and studied her, his gaze tracking from her eyes to her mouth and back. "Okay, Red. Tell me again why this isn't going to work."

"Because neither of us wants to risk jeopardizing our relationship with Maeve over...anything. We both know better than to think we could keep our relationship with each other separate from our relationship with her. And I've lost people after relationships ended before—people I really cared about."

She'd never forget what it had been like to go from being embraced as the daughter Paul's mother never had, to realizing the same woman was walking out of the market without her groceries to avoid having to talk to her. The friends who suddenly hadn't seen her when they passed. That feeling of being cast adrift from everything she'd thought was safe and secure.

When she'd transferred to Chicago for a fresh start Maeve had been the one to give it to her. Maeve's had been the open heart she'd so desperately needed after having so many others shut against her.

When it looked like Garrett might be ready to argue Nichole held up a staying finger. "And because I think you're a very good guy. I know too much about the part of you that has nothing to do with whispering panties and everything to do with the care and protection of your family. I know about the guy who drives around Chicago at five in the morning after a big snow to dig out his sisters' cars so they can drive to work. The guy who puts his own needs last every time. And the guy who knows the value of a simple sunset."

"Are you whispering *me* right now?"

Nichole shook her head, half wishing she was. "No, I'm telling you why this won't work. It's because you're too good of a guy for me not to fall for. I'm not ready for something serious and I don't know how to do casual. Believe it or not, that's actually how your name came up with Maeve. She'd been joking around about you giving me lessons on keeping it light. She even threatened to set us up. Ironic, huh?"

When Nichole looked up from the neat stack of her hands on her knees Garrett was watching her, his brows drawn down so his shadowed eyes left her guessing at his reaction.

"So what are we going to do about this...*thing* between us?"

"What we planned from the start. Ignore it." She let out a soft laugh. "Find a distraction until it goes away. Because us getting together would be a mistake and I think we both know it."

"Okay, Nichole. I get it." Garrett pushed to his feet and, taking her hand, pulled her to her own.

Looking down at where their fingers had intertwined, she asked, "No more whispering?"

One last rough stroke of his thumb across her knuckles and he let her go. "Not tonight."

EIGHT

Garrett gripped the wheel, ten and two, his knuckles going white as his most beloved baby sister rambled on, heedless of how close she was to being dumped by the side of a road and left to hoof it the rest of the way to Carla's in the next burb over.

"...all I'm saying is you don't have to be such a hard-ass about everything all the time—sorry, Aunt Gloria."

Their great-aunt waved a papery hand, her focus on the passing houses more than on the fight Maeve had picked with him the moment she'd slid into the backseat.

"You think I like this? That I enjoy always being the heavy? Come on, Maeve. If I don't tell Erin to turn her head on and open her eyes about this guy then who the hell will? You? Beth? Carla? I don't think so. You girls are so caught up in all the romance B.S. you don't even register the impracticality of a guy who literally weaves baskets for a living."

"He's an artist," she sniped back.

"Oh, he *is*. Everyone was talking about how beautiful his work was at the Acres."

The seniors' living facility where his latest works were on sale.

Maeve's eyes narrowed and she crossed her arms over her chest. "It doesn't matter what he does, Garrett. Erin loves him."

At his scoff, she grumbled from the back, "And to think I'd been looking forward to seeing you. Where have you been anyway?"

He made some noise about work and scowled at the road ahead, not wanting to get into it. But Maeve was...*Maeve*.

"Cripes, it's either feast or famine with you. Years of you only pulling your head out of your business and books long enough to bitch about whatever we're doing wrong, and then suddenly you're like a plague. Everywhere." Her eyes rolled as she let out a dramatic huff. "And just when I start thinking it was kind of fun having you around, you drop off the face of the earth again."

Teeth gritting down, he glanced in the mirror at her. "You've managed fine in the past."

"Yeah, but I always had Nichole around. And she's been suspiciously absent these last couple weeks. Tired. Busy. Working late."

Garrett's hands tightened on the wheel as the implication hung in the air.

Damn it.

"Anything you want to own up to?"

Not even close. "No."

The silence stretched between them until finally he shot a demanding look into the rearview mirror. "What?"

"I thought you liked her."

"I do." More than he should, considering what he had to offer.

"You know, Garrett, I've always wanted a sister."

Wonderful. And now she was playing with him for sport. Because that was what demon sisters did.

Breathe. Don't start looking for a ditch. "You have three."

"But not a *little* sister. You know Nikki is two months younger than I am?"

"It's not like that, Maeve."

Gloria's frail hand reached up through the seats to pinch his cheek. "It's wonderful, dear. All your wild-oat sowing has to stop sometime. Nikki's a darling girl."

Another reminder that Nichole was in with his entire family. Including his great-aunt.

"It's not like that," he said again, though why he bothered he had no idea.

"So what's it like, then, Big Brother?"

Did he really want to have this conversation? Only a glance into the back showed that both women, despite their respective teasing and maternal pats, were intent on getting the scoop. And maybe saying it out loud would help it finally sink in.

"I don't want to marry her."

Maeve barked out an indignant cough. "Geez, I didn't realize she'd asked."

Snide. Nice.

"She didn't. Obviously. But—" Damn it, he'd wanted to get that critical tidbit out first, because it seemed important. But the way it landed he sounded like an ass. For more than one reason. Cue the clarifications. "I'm just trying to explain. It isn't because she isn't good enough. She is. I mean, I can't believe either of those schmucks she was engaged to let her get away. Any guy would be lucky to have her. Trust me when I tell you I *want* to have her. Just not in the way she deserves."

"It's okay," Maeve offered from the backseat. "You've had an overfull plate for a long time. And after Mom and Dad you have a hard time letting people in. Getting close. You aren't ready to think about marriage yet."

He bristled, not for the first time cursing Maeve's freshman-year psychology class.

It wasn't about letting people get close. Or what had happened with his parents.

True, he didn't have a lot of people outside Jesse and his sisters he shared much of a bond with. But that had more to do with what his life had been like these last years than any avoidance on his part. And the connection with Nichole had been immediate. She was the person he'd become *most* comfortable talking to.

It was about things like this damn recurring conversation about Erin's boyfriend. He'd been playing the "hard-ass" and making tough calls for over half his life already, and what he wanted out of a relationship was something where those kinds of responsibilities didn't apply. Where the consequences of his actions and choices didn't impact the rest of another person's life.

Hell, just thinking about it had the muscles in his gut starting to knot.

"It's not just *yet*. I don't know if I'm going to want it *ever*. Which makes me a bum deal for a woman with 'someday' in mind." His fingers tightened around the wheel. "Nichole's been engaged twice. She's a woman with a white picket fence dream just waiting to be realized."

Maeve sat back in her seat, arms crossed in a contemplative pose. "I don't know, Garrett. Yeah, she's going to want to get married eventually. But I think for now Nikki just needs to learn how to have a little fun again. And from what I hear...you're a pretty fun guy."

He let out a humorless laugh, not feeling like much fun at all. "But not the guy for Nichole."

They'd decided already. They weren't going to pursue it. And the problem wasn't just an off alignment of goals...it was also the little lady sitting in the seat behind him. It was the strings.

Maeve's lips pursed as she stared him down.

"And you're cool with that?"

"Yep." No. But he'd get there.

"Just as well. There are a lot of fun guys out there. And her dance card is filling up anyway."

Sure...right...wait— "What?"

Only Maeve seemed to have lost interest in him and turned to Gloria.

"So, yesterday two guys from her office asked her out. Within an hour of each other..."

Of course they had. Because she was gorgeous. And she'd probably had that smile going—the one that stuck with a guy for days after he'd seen it. The kind of smile that made a guy want to get to the bottom of what exactly put it there and make sure—

"And you know Nikki—she's always with the flat-out forget it, but in that really smooth way she's got. Probably because she doesn't even realize it's going on most of the time. But this time—"

A horn blared and Garrett jerked the wheel. Hell.

"Geez, Garrett. Take it easy. Precious cargo back here."

"Sorry, girls." He needed to get his head together. But, damn, Maeve needed to knock off the dish...or get to the point a hell of a lot faster.

Only now his great-aunt Gloria was tapping at the window. "Oh, would you look at this house?"

Maeve nodded her approval. "I love the landscaping."

Garrett did a mental ten count, willing his heart rate to slow, his blood to cool. There was no way Maeve was going to leave them hanging, was there? And even if she'd seriously lost her train of thought how was it his aunt wasn't demanding resolution?

"My roses never bloom like that. I've added eggshells, coffee grounds."

"Maybe it's got to do with the sun or how much water they get."

"Nichole," Garrett barked out, fast on his way to losing his cool. "What did she do?"

Silence from the back of the car. He checked the mirror and found both Maeve and Gloria staring at him. One looking quietly amused, the other looking... satisfied.

"What did she do when, Garrett?"

Molars grinding down, he shot a look at his baby sister he hadn't been forced to use since she was sixteen. A look that seemed to have lost its mojo, based on the way she crossed her arms and jutted her chin at him.

"You mean with all the guys asking her out?"

Now it was *all the guys*? The steering wheel creaked within his grasp and he forced his grip looser. "Yes."

Maeve checked her nails. "She hadn't decided when I talked to her. But she did say a date might be just the distraction she needed."

The car slammed to a stop and he stared out the windshield at his sister's driveway. The front door opened and relatives streamed out to greet them, but Garrett just cranked around in his seat. "A distraction?"

Maeve blanched, leaning back in her seat as Gloria shuffled out of the car.

"I'm sure she didn't mean it...however it is you're taking it."

Except Garrett was damn sure she did. Which meant she was still as hung up as he was.

And she was about to look to another guy to distract her.

"Out of the car, Maeve."

NINE

—

Knock, knock, knock. Knock, knock.

Nichole swallowed hard, her heart beating like the fist at her door.

Garrett.

Maeve's single cryptic text had been the only warning. No explanation of what he wanted. No response when she'd texted back. And now, after two weeks of avoiding him, of lying awake at night thinking about the hard crush of his mouth and the low rumble of his voice, of telling herself just a few more days and she'd get past this physio-emotional chaos she'd never expected herself to be a part of, he was here.

She didn't have to answer. She could walk back to her room. Turn out the lights and lie in bed until the sun came up the next day. It didn't matter that Garrett had seen the light in her windows and knew she was home. It wasn't as though he wouldn't understand what she was doing. He might not even blame her.

So why wasn't she turning around and walking back

down the hall? Why wasn't she flipping off the lights and climbing into her bed alone?

Because it would be rude? Because he'd spent the last forty minutes driving back from a family party he hadn't even made it inside for to see her? Because maybe they needed to talk around an issue they'd already beaten to death?

No.

The answer lay in the nervous flutter deep in her belly. In the almost painful thump of her heart. In the eager ache that had permeated her body as a whole.

She *wanted* him.

Like she couldn't remember wanting anything before.

Fingers trembling, she reached for the door. Felt the pull of him like a loose charge in the air even as she grounded herself against the knob. And then the door was swinging open and there was Garrett with those deep blue whirlpool eyes coming up to meet hers as his lips slanted into a grin.

This was such a mistake.

One solid arm was braced against the frame above her head as he reached for the back of her neck and leaned in, stopping only a breath away. "I hear you need a *distraction*."

Ah-ha.

Now she understood. Maeve had repeated something only Garrett could fully understand. And he hadn't liked what he'd heard.

Heat rushed her cheeks and, wetting her lips, she

tried to think of something to say. Only the rough growl of approval as his eyes followed the movement blanked her mind of anything beyond how glad she was to see him…and how wrong that was.

She looked up into his eyes. "I keep thinking about you."

A nod. She could feel his breath swirling over the side of her face.

"Same here."

"I thought—" She swallowed, tried not to lean into all the heat of a body too close to ignore. "Giving someone else a chance might help."

The fingers at the back of her neck stroked, soft and gentle. "So you've got a date?"

And yet there was no mistaking the firm hold for anything but the possessive claim it was.

"No. I backed out." It wouldn't be fair to go out with one man solely in the hopes of his distracting her from another. Especially when the likelihood of it working was so slim.

"Good."

God, those eyes. The feel of him so close. Her body hummed in response to his proximity. What were they going to do about this?

"So I've got an idea."

Nichole nodded. She was starting to get an idea as well. One night. The night they never should have left unfinished all those weeks ago. Finally out of their systems. And then they'd never get within fifty feet of each other again. It wouldn't interfere with her relationship with Maeve. It wouldn't threaten anything.

"I like it," she murmured, pressing her palms into the broad chest too temptingly close to ignore.

Garrett let out a gruff laugh, then tipped her head back to bring her attention up to his eyes. "I'm glad. But how about you hear it first, then agree?"

Was she really going to do this?

A look into those eyes burning with a need that matched her own—yes. Definitely.

One night. It was all she needed.

"Tell me." Her palms skimmed downward, riding the dips and valleys of his abdomen.

"We give Maeve's plan a go."

That caught her attention. Chin pulling back, she shook off the haze of need and focused on the man before her. "What?"

"You say you don't know how to do casual. And I don't know how to do anything else. So we meet in the middle. Find some safe place that feels good. That's about having some fun instead of forever. I'm thinking, for a while, we could be friends and lovers. We'd trust each other not to let it go too far and just...learn to date."

For a while. Not one night.

She let out a heavy breath.

"Garrett, I don't think you're the right guy to practice dating with. You were right about the strings. Those complications matter."

"I'm the perfect guy. And the only string I see is the

one Maeve keeps dangling in front of me—the one with *you on the end*. She's not going to flip when this is over. She's a big girl. And she's your best friend, so give her some credit."

Nichole's mouth dropped open in shock. *Garrett* was telling *her* to give Maeve some credit?

"You've got to be kidding?"

Garrett shook his head, brought his thumb around to stroke across her bottom lip.

Oh, God. Such slight contact...but with an earth-shattering impact.

"Not even close. And, to underscore my point, I'm going to give you your first lesson in keeping it casual." Those deep blue pools were pulling her deeper. The gravel-rough voice was like a siren song, luring her to depths she shouldn't go. "Don't make things more complicated than they need to be. Neither one of us wants this to get too serious. So it won't. Simple."

"Easy for The Panty Whisperer to say." His thumb was still at her lip, offering that tantalizing sensation with every word.

"Easy for anyone on the same page to say." He ducked down so his eyes were level with hers. "And you're the perfect woman for me because I need more, Nichole. More than the kind of meaningless that's been on tap for longer than I want to remember. But my *more* has a pretty hard limit when it comes to the future. And you might be the only woman I trust not to try and change that. Don't you see? Right now, at this place in our lives, we're a perfect fit."

She wanted to believe him. Wanted it to be that easy. But sometimes things didn't go the way people planned. Sometimes the best intentions led to the worst kinds of hurt. And she was afraid.

He leaned closer then, so his words slid around her ear in warm rush. "*Trust me, Nichole.*"

Trust. He was asking her to trust him. To trust Maeve. To trust herself.

Could she do it?

If she ever wanted a full life she had to learn how.

And this man she wanted so desperately understood so much about her.

Knuckles coasting down the length of her neck, Garrett murmured, "Trust me to take care of you."

Her breath caught as he pulled back to look down at her, the dark promise in his eyes enough to make her belly twist in on itself.

Her lips parted on what might have a warning to herself, or maybe just his name because she loved the feel of it on her tongue—but he was already there. Closing those last scant inches between them and catching her mouth with his kiss.

She was lost. No more denials. No more waiting.

Arms snaked around her back, he pulled her close, taking her weight as he took her self-control. He carried her inside and kicked the door closed behind them.

Feet dangling above the floor, she reveled in the strength of his embrace, the power of his need. The ever-tightening hold that roared they'd waited too long already and threatened nothing short of *everything* would be enough.

Her arms laced around his neck, pulling him closer, because after telling herself no for so long this was finally *yes*.

He walked them down the hall toward her room, deepening the kiss as they went. Taking the access she offered and thrusting inside. Retreating and then sliding past her lips again, slow and steady. Telling her what he wanted to do to her without words. Filling her mouth with the rough stroke of his tongue, the taste of him. Decadent and delicious.

Yes!

He thrust again and she closed around him, sucking softly in an urgent, needy plea. Begging him for more. For all.

He pressed into her hips, so the steely thick ridge of his erection nudged firm against her belly. It was a hint. A taunt. A tease that left her whimpering as she tried to squirm closer. Take what she needed.

And then her back was against the wall and his hands were sliding across her bottom, strong fingers splaying wide as they pushed down the backs of her thighs past the hem of her sundress. Each point of contact became a bruising demand as they guided her legs around him, positioning her so his hot length met her center with a rolling pressure just exactly right.

"Garrett—oh, God, like that," she gasped, her words taking on an insistent quality, warning of a total loss of control.

Garrett did it again and again until desire lanced her core.

Her legs tightened with her fists in his hair, and the low growl vibrating between them was his. "I need to get inside you, baby."

His hands released their hold on her hips, letting her legs slip down the heavy slabs of his thighs until her feet touched the floor.

"Yes, please." Her eyes were trailing up and down his body, her mind plotting the fastest way to rid him of his clothes, working justifications on which ones weren't critical in the removal process. Because really all she needed was him sitting on that bed, his fly open and boxers pushed down. *Oh, God.*

A shudder ripped through her at the mental image alone.

Glancing over her shoulder, she saw they were mere feet from her room. Her bed. From her half-clothed, full-penetration, hard-and-fast-and-finally fantasy.

Dragging her eyes back to his, she whispered, "I can't wait anymore."

She pulled at Garrett's belt with greedy, shaking hands and, unbuckling it, used the tongue to lead him the rest of the way.

At her bed, she caught the sides of her skirt in each hand and pulled the dress over her head, tossing it to the floor.

Garrett froze, his own shirt caught over one shoulder as he stared down at her, naked but for white cotton bikini panties.

Her thumbs pushed into the delicate waistband, pushing them down.

Fabric ripped and buttons bounced across the floor, followed by the tattered remnants of Garrett's shirt. The denim of his jeans put up a better defense, but soon it too was piled in a heap and her back was hitting the mattress as Garrett followed her down, kissing her hard all the way, his body covering hers in a tease of flesh against flesh before he broke away to sheath himself.

And then his thick head was nudging at her opening as his blue eyes held with hers. All the urgency and frantic need slipped away as, slowly, he pushed inside. Easing in and out by incremental degrees as her body stretched to accommodate the greater size of his. The cost of his restraint and his care was etched in all the lines of his face until, at last, he sank deep, filling the snug hold of her body.

Her lips parted on a fragile gasp that was decadent torture and supreme satisfaction all in one. So totally, incomparably worth the wait.

She wanted to stay like that forever, with him buried so thick and deep within her that she felt his every breath and heartbeat in the most intimate, erotic way—something Garrett seemed to be in agreement with as he held himself on straightened arms, staring down into her eyes with a look that made her feel like the sunset he'd waited years to see.

Without thought her hands went to his face, the

light stubble a tender scrape beneath her fingers. "You're every fantasy I never dared to dream."

Garrett's smile was satisfied and wanting all at once. "I don't think you have enough fantasies, sweetheart."

"Then maybe you'll give me some more."

His hips began to move and his eyes took on an intensity she never could have fathomed. "Starting now, Nichole."

Nichole collapsed on the bed. Her limbs weak and useless. Her mind spinning over the events of the last few hours.

Even now her belly curled in and on to itself at the memory. So. Unbelievably. Good.

The kind of *good* a girl could get used to. Spoiled by. Caught up in.

Summoning all her strength, she turned her head on her pillow to look at Garrett, who'd collapsed beside her. He was staring at the ceiling, his breath working in and out of his chest in ragged draws.

He really *had* done most of the work.

She thought back to the chair. Maybe seventy-five percent.

The hallway. Okay, eighty-five. God, that had been so good.

And she must have purred her approval too, because Garrett's brows edged up as he looked over at her, that arrogantly satisfied smile stamped across his mouth. "Something on your mind?"

No sense in denying it. "The hall."

His lids went to half-mast. His voice even lower. *"The hall."*

And then he was reaching for her, pulling her in with arms so big and strong she felt as though she were thin as a wisp and lighter than air rather than the flesh-and-blood real woman she was. Another decadent sensation.

Leaning in to taste her lips once, then once more, but this time slow and lingering with a low, rumbling groan finish, Garrett looked deeply into her eyes.

"So there's something I'd like to try, if you're up for it. You know—feeling...experimental and all." His gaze dropped to her mouth. "It's something I've never done before."

Nichole blinked, thoughts of the last handful of hours running through her mind like a PowerPoint presentation for Experimental 101.

Something even *Garrett* hadn't tried?

Her heart skipped and a flutter of genuine nerves pulled her too-loose limbs back into working order. "Um...I'm not saying no...yet. But...um...Garrett, what exactly are you talking about...*exactly?*"

He pulled her closer still, so she ended up lying on top of him, and let out a long breath. "Seriously, only if you're into it, Nichole. Only if you really think you can handle it."

She swallowed. "Just tell me."

Garrett drew her head toward his and whispered in

her ear, "I'd like to spend the night. Stay. Sleep here with you."

Nichole reared back, planting her hands over his wide chest and tucking her knees at either side of his ribs.

"You!" She laughed on a rush of breath. "I can't believe you—you know what—" But then all she could do was laugh, looking down into Mr. All-Innocence's smirking face. "You're bad."

Hands coasting up her bare legs, over her hips and back down again, he answered, "Like there was ever any question... But maybe not quite as bad as you assumed."

"No. Not at all." The teasing fell away and reality settled around her. He was asking her for something serious, disguising it behind laughter and games.

"You've really never slept over at a woman's place before?"

"No."

This time it wasn't nerves running through her but something else. Something warmer. Something she was certain was still just this side of okay in terms of the whole caring-while-keeping-it-casual deal they'd struck.

Leaning forward, so this time she was the one whispering in his ear, she said, "Don't worry. Since this is your first time I promise to be gentle."

TEN

Garrett leaned back against Nichole's kitchen counter, the sound and smell of brewing coffee filling the air around him. He'd woken at five, like he normally did, only to discover there was nothing normal about this morning.

He wasn't in his apartment. And not crashed out on one of his sisters' couches or spare beds either. But still in the delectable Nichole's bed and completely wrapped around her.

And, damn, if that hadn't felt good.

A little too good, based on the way he'd been pressed hard against her back.

He'd entertained a handful of fun-and-games kind of wake-up scenarios, most of which involved getting his tongue all over her before she quite knew what was doing. But they'd only actually gone to sleep about three hours before. And, while *his* internal alarm wouldn't cut him any slack, if Nichole could catch the extra Zs she should.

He didn't want her nodding off at the wheel or letting her body wear down.

Figuring he'd pass on worrying about all the what-ifs of Nichole not getting enough rest, he'd climbed out of bed—mindful of the woman still sleeping there.

Now he was milling around her kitchen, waiting for the coffee to brew...making a mental list of repairs the place needed. The hinge on the cabinet door. The track on the silverware drawer.

He'd be willing to bet she'd like a new counter. One of those granite slabs to replace the tile she had.

And then there was the fact that he didn't need to be taking over the maintenance of Nichole's place. What was he *doing*?

She didn't need this from him. And he didn't need—

"Hey."

Garrett turned around and all thoughts about replacing a segment of the baseboard or not were temporarily shelved as he looked to where Nichole stood on the threshold of the kitchen, wrapped up in one of those stretchy thin robes that didn't actually look all that warm...and, so far as he could tell, nothing else.

"Hey, yourself. Hope you don't mind I started a pot?"

Her mouth pulled to one side as she finger-combed a few wild curls from her face. "You're asking me if I mind that you made coffee, but not that you've pried up a piece of my floor?"

He looked down at where his Swiss Army knife was wedged between the wall and—and *hell*. Looking back at Nichole, he offered the only defense he had. "I'm good at fixing things. And it's just the baseboard. The floor beneath looks fine."

Shuffling into the kitchen, Nichole just nodded at him, looking adorably exhausted as she folded herself into a kitchen chair and then tried to cover an enormous yawn with her small hand.

"Okay, but your kind is notorious for taking things apart and leaving them that way. Indefinitely. Anything you touch in this place gets put back to rights within the week." She slanted a look at him. "Regardless of whether this thing with us has run its course."

Giving them less than a week to run their course? Grumpy, grumpy. She didn't need to worry about his taking her place apart piece by piece. It was a habit, but one he intended to kick. With Nichole, he didn't want to be the guy who had to fix everything.

Okay, he'd fix the baseboard...because now that he'd seen it, the damn thing would nag at the back of his mind until he knew it was taken care of. But that was it.

Garrett looked between Nichole and the coffee. After the baseboard, the only thing he'd fix for Nichole was a hot cup of joe. Grabbing a mug from the tree beside the pot, he poured her a cup. "Cream? Sugar?"

A smile flickered at the corner of her mouth as she looked him up and down. "Whipped cream."

With a shrug, he turned for the fridge, but Nichole was already up and walking over. "Thank you, Garrett, but I'll get it dressed up. I'm kind of particular."

"Sure." Even better.

He watched her navigating her space, seeing a routine he never would have thought to imagine, liking the look of her in the morning in this environment that so few would have the opportunity to experience.

Possessive satisfaction swelled within him at the thought, urging him into closer contact. His fingers played through her hair as she topped off her coffee with skim milk, swirled a spoon through the pale brew and then clinked it at the side of the mug twice.

Another sideways glance and she was looking very amused. "So, was it...*good for you?*"

The overnight.

Giving in to the laugh Nichole always seemed to pull from him, he nodded. "Very."

"Seriously, how is it you've never spent the night with a woman before?"

Garrett took her hand and led her over to the breakfast nook by the bay window and, setting down his own coffee rather than giving up the loose hold he had on her fingers, pulled out her chair. "It just always seemed more of a complication than it would be worth."

But then, he hadn't exactly known what he was missing.

Parking it across the table, he threw back half his own mug—more about the infusion of caffeine than the lingering warmth he'd take his time over on the next cup.

"Really?" she asked, pulling her feet up beneath her

as she settled in. "I guess I would have thought in some ways making a getaway would be more complicated."

Nichole brought the mug to her lips and took a long swallow, her satisfaction all too distracting. But she'd asked a question. And, though the answer wasn't exactly simple, he trusted her with it.

"Not really. I mean, at first it just wasn't an option. I didn't go off to college at eighteen like most of the other guys did, so it wasn't like I could just sneak some co-ed into my dorm. I was living at home with my four sisters. Basically raising them."

"Wait—Bethany's a year older than you, and wasn't your mom still around? I mean weren't there times you could have got away if you'd wanted to? Weren't there co-eds trying to sneak you into their dorms?"

Sure there were. Truth be told, there had been for years. "Yeah, but there was a lot going on. Our situation at home was pretty precarious for a number of reasons. My parents hadn't done a lot of contingency planning. There was a small policy that got us through the first couple years, but my mom didn't work, and I didn't want the girls' futures to die with my dad. Bethany was smart as hell. Always making those gifted programs at school. A hell of a lot more going on than I ever had, that's for sure. And with the earning potential in the house pretty well limited to what I could eke out, her grades were her ticket into college. So that was her job and she nailed it. Free ride right through."

Nichole was smiling at him then, and he knew she'd

seen the pride he couldn't contain when it came to his older sister.

"Which was great, but it meant she was basically gone by the time I was seventeen." He'd never been a senior in high school, because by then he'd dropped out to work full-time. Everyone had helped out in the day-to-day—but the money, the bills, keeping the house fixed up had fallen to Garrett.

"My mom had always been kind of fragile. I have no idea how she managed to have five kids, but even before Dad died we'd all become pretty adept at chipping in. Which is probably the only reason we were able to make it the way we did. She never really recovered from losing him."

"Garrett, that must have been so hard."

He nodded, closing his eyes. And for a moment he was back in his kitchen that day, with some textbook open in front of him, his dad blowing through the room with all his endless energy, trailing a bunch of little girls clamoring for a last kiss before he took off for work. He'd leaned over Garrett and looked at the page, shaking his head in that bewildered way he'd had when it came to school.

He'd been blue-collar to the core. Working in construction from his teens. No higher education. Just a salt-of-the-earth, meat-and-potatoes man's man who'd loved his family.

He'd clapped Garrett on the shoulder and nodded toward his wife over at the counter, cleaning up breakfast. "You're the man of the house while I'm gone, son. Make me proud."

Same words every day. And Garrett had grinned, rolling his eyes at the idea. Still, he always gave his dad his everyday commitment—"Yes, sir"—earning that last, "Good kid," as he left for work.

Thirty minutes later his father had been dead. And all Garrett had had to honor the man he'd worshipped was that last promise he'd made.

Clearing his throat, he looked back at Nichole. "Mom tried. She got meals on the table and held it together enough so, for a while, the relatives weren't asking questions. But even as kids we had a sort of instinctual understanding of her limitations. She cried a lot. Spent more and more time in her room. Less and less time doing the things a capable parent did. If there was a crisis in the middle of the night she wasn't the one the girls went to. It was me. And by the end— when I was eighteen—it got to where she needed the kind of help she couldn't get at home. Hell, she should have had help before then, but we— I just didn't understand."

The guilt inexorably tied to thoughts of his mother pushed at him, weighing in his gut and chest. The question that never went away... If he'd gotten her help earlier would she have had a chance?

"My God, Garrett, I'm so sorry. I didn't realize your mother— Maeve doesn't talk a lot about her."

It didn't surprise him. "Maeve missed out on the most Mom had to give. She was just a little kid. And it was tough to lose so much at once. It was tough on all of them, but we got through it. And, long story short, someone needed to be around. I sure as hell didn't like the idea of my sisters being alone overnight, you know?"

There were just too many things that could happen...and he'd thought about *all* of them.

Nichole's brow pushed up. "That being the case, how in the world did you ever get this Panty Whisperer reputation?"

"I was a teenager." He laughed. "With *needs*. No privacy at home. And a *very* short window of free time every other week or so to take care of them. Thank God I had a few friends with older sisters who were willing to be the responsible party and babysit once in a while."

"So you're citing your libido as an example of necessity being the mother of invention?"

"Exactly." Then he held up a hand. "Only I don't want it to sound like I was one of those guys who'd say anything to get into a girl's pants. I wasn't."

She laughed, shaking her head. "I'm guessing you probably wouldn't need to, Garrett."

But then her eyes found his again and they were still serious. Still waiting.

"What about later, though? After you got Maeve and the rest through school and out on their own? What about then?"

"By then I'd taken over running the construction company and I was going after my own degree. Still not a lot of free time. But, yeah, obviously I could have spent some of it crashed out overnight in a woman's bed. It just seemed smarter not to."

"Afraid they'd get ideas?"

"Yes." It sounded bad. But all he had was the truth. "It was important to me that the women I took out didn't get the wrong idea about what was happening. About what *could* happen."

He hadn't had the time to get to know them well enough to figure out if he could trust them to take his word for the kinds of limits a relationship with him would have. And so his romantic interactions had always been sort of stunted, shallow exercises that served a specific need.

Until Nichole.

Because not only did he finally have the time, but she already knew the score. She already knew him better than any other woman he'd ever taken out. They had honesty and communication on their side.

And the freedom in that—just to be together and enjoy what they were doing—was incredible.

There was only one problem. He hadn't actually taken Nichole *out* at all.

If ever there was a woman who deserved a solid date from him it was this one. But so far he'd picked her up at a party, literally picked her up in the back of a coffee shop and backed her into her place with no intention of letting her out until he'd gotten her to...well, where he'd gotten her. Several times, he mentally amended, giving into a satisfied grin.

"What's that look about?" Nichole asked, cuddling her coffee mug to her chest.

"I was just thinking about where I should take you for our first date."

ELEVEN

———

"You can't be serious." Nichole laughed, trying to keep up as Garrett half-towed her through a parking lot toward what appeared to be some kind of two-dimensional enchanted castle ahead.

"Why not? This is our first date—*official* first date. Because the weeknight dinners don't count and I actually *called* you in advance to set this one up—so it seemed appropriate."

God, she loved that he was so into giving them a first date. Even if they *had* spent five of the last six nights together, with Garrett proving to her time and time again what a stellar decision it had been going forward with a relationship.

Giving her hand a squeeze, he added, "And it's on my bucket list."

Nichole ground to a stop, thinking she'd never get used to the things that came out of this man's mouth. "Your bucket list?"

"Yeah." He brushed a strand of flyaway hair back

from her face, tucking it behind her ear. "The stuff you want to do before you die."

"I know what it is. I'm just surprised to learn miniature golf makes yours." The idea of him trying to navigate that big body through a tiny maze of six-foot fairways was just too much.

"Why? Because it's such good clean fun?" Leaning in, he let his voice take on a conspiratorial tone. "If helping me live out one of my adolescent fantasies is too wholesome for you we could always make it a little more *interesting...*"

Her heart skipped a beat as she met his hot gaze. "You want to wager?"

"Why not? We could come up with some creative terms." Wrapping that powerful arm around her shoulders, he guided them toward the main entrance. "And I've never played before...so your chances of winning are about as good as they're going to get."

She'd been hearing Maeve talk about this guy for years. He was relentlessly competitive. And a natural at most everything he put his mind to trying. Which meant, regardless of his experience, there was a good chance she wasn't going to win. "What kind of terms?"

The hot glint in Garrett's eyes had her belly tightening and nervous excitement zinging across the surface of her skin.

Five minutes later Nichole was intimately acquainted with the business end of Garrett's brawn. The side of him that had made him the perfect candidate to move out of heavy lifting and take over his mentor's construction company. He was a guy who liked to negotiate, and he wasn't above a little hard-ball when it came to getting his outrageous terms laid down in lead on the back of the scorecard. And she liked that side of him too.

Who was she kidding? She liked everything about him.

The way he took her by surprise and caught her off guard. His first dates. His soulful reflections. His naughty wish-lists. He was just so much more than she'd expected. More than she'd been prepared for.

So much more...that there were moments when quiet alarms began to sound in the back of her mind. But then she'd catch his eye and see all that steady confidence shining out at her, and she'd remember they knew what they were doing. That this was safe. And she'd just give in to all the incredible feel-good that was being with Garrett.

She trusted him.

Or at least she *had*.

One mini-golf slaughter later, Nichole was flopped over the wide slab of Garrett's shoulder, one hand fisted around his belt, the other clinging to his back pocket, as the hard, cold truth washed over her.

She'd been hustled.

Outraged, incensed and entirely too charmed by his betrayal, she charged, "You told me you'd never played before!"

"I haven't," he answered, those long legs striding through the now mostly empty parking lot. "But I've got a knack for picking new things up. Especially when there's an incentive on the line."

Then, in typical Garrett fashion, with a hand behind her head to ensure she didn't bump it, he set her into the car.

"And the backseat is on your bucket list too?"

He at least had the good sense to look chagrined. "No. But having to work my way into your panties is."

"I think you know just exactly how willing I am. How willing we've *all* been."

He hushed her with a warm breath at her ear. "Come on. I won. You've got to play hard-to-get."

She backed further across the bench seat, heat pouring through her center as it did every other time Garrett looked at her the way he was looking at her right then.

He wanted to have to work for her, did he?

"I'm not sure I should let you anywhere near me after the stunt you just pulled."

The satisfaction shining out of those half-lidded blues was almost enough for her to throw down any pretense at resistance and haul him into the seat beside her. Better yet, on top of her.

But he wanted to play. And playing was something she'd never had enough practice with. So here, in the far corner of a darkened parking lot, Nichole was ready to prioritize fun.

As Garrett wrapped one strong hand around the seat-back beside her, hefting himself into a space too small to accommodate him, she offered the most skeptical, resistant look she could muster. "I'm not sure about this, Garrett."

His answering deep-chested groan promised her feigned hard-to-get was hitting the right note. That and the hell-yes glint in his eyes.

"Oh, come on, Nichole," he cajoled. "I promise. I just want to talk. That's all."

Yeah, her too. Right. "Maybe...just for a minute."

Nichole had been prepared for the questions. She was out with Maeve, Bethany and Erin for their usual girls' night dinner...and she'd been dating their brother in an official public capacity for three weeks now.

Sure, Maeve had been giving her a good grilling on and off since the very first night. But apparently she'd been holding back. Storing up for tonight.

It was almost laughable—except there was something way too serious in the three sets of eyes watching her from across the mostly cleared table. And she was getting a very one-against-three vibe.

"But you guys got arrested together!"

Shaking her head, she shot Maeve a murderous look. "I told you—they didn't even take us in."

Maeve did the whole shoulders-around-her-ears thing while she dabbed at the corner of her mouth with her napkin. "And I told you I wouldn't say anything. But apparently you didn't secure the same blood oath from Officer Klinsky...who happened to be in Carla's class. And ran into one of her girlfriends at the video store yesterday. Sordid tales travel fast, honey."

Bethany grinned from behind her wineglass. "But thank you for confirming a story I hadn't believed."

Perfect.

Erin's mouth was doing one of those weird twitchy things that happened when someone was trying exceptionally hard to keep a straight face. Not happening. Not even close.

Leaning an elbow on the table, Nichole laid her napkin to the side of her plate. "Just spit it out. I can see you've got something good."

Wicked laughter that was totally Carter family burst past her lips as she glanced from one sister to the other and then back to Nichole. "Can you see the invitations? Embossed with bars? A pair of handcuffs between their names?"

All three Carter girls broke into gales of laughter, but suddenly Nichole didn't feel like laughing. Invitations. *Wedding* invitations.

Just the kind of place she didn't want her mind to go.

And then, to make matters worse, she had the sudden certain sense they weren't alone. Sure enough, within seconds a wide hand was warming her shoulder and another Carter's deeper, darker and yet just as playful voice was joining in with the rest. "I thought I recognized those cackles."

A chorus of delighted welcome sounded around the table as Garrett made the rounds, dropping a kiss at each sister's cheek as he went. An endearing habit which had Nichole smiling despite the fact her number-one taboo topic had been introduced mere seconds before.

Had Garrett heard?

Everything was going so well between them. The relationship was staying neatly within the lines they'd drawn. And it all felt so good. She didn't want anything...anyone...to jeopardize it. But one glance around the table and she knew without a shadow of a doubt there was no way Garrett wasn't going to get an earful about their brush with the law and what a special theme it would make, come marriage-time.

She almost wanted to drag him away to the nearest back hall for one last walk on the *Garrett side* before she had to let him go.

"What are you doing, crashing our girls' night out?" Bethany asked, clearly delighted to see her brother.

Garrett nodded toward the plate-glass window across the dining room. "Had a dinner meeting at the place down the street. Was heading to catch a cab when I happened to look in and see this table of lovely ladies. Don't worry, I won't stay. Just wanted to say hello and make sure you were all getting enough to eat."

At that moment the waiter arrived, hefting a tray laden with every dessert on the menu. None of which they'd ordered. "Compliments of the gentleman."

"Dinner's on me, girls." He grinned as his sisters chirped out delighted thank-yous and then started staking claims on which decadent tart, chocolate pot or indulgent wedge of cake they wanted to try first.

Nichole took his hand and, when he met her eyes, mouthed a thank-you of her own.

He winked, giving her a squeeze. "Enjoy the evening and don't do anything rumor suggests I might do."

At that, Bethany threatened tears if he didn't join them, and when everyone joined in he happily relented, taking a seat beside Nichole.

"So—having a good night, girls?"

There was really no way to warn him.

"The best, Garrett," Erin assured him. "But not as good a night as it sounds like *you* had two weeks ago."

Nichole had to give him credit. The guy didn't bat an eye or let on in any way he was squirming. And if she hadn't caught the ever so slight darkening across his cheekbones she might not have known at all. But there it was. *Red.*

And for once it wasn't her.

"Apparently the cop knows Carla," she offered helpfully.

And then Erin dropped the bomb, sharing her fabulous ideas on an arrest-themed wedding.

Nichole had expected Garrett's reaction to be something along the lines of a sudden silence. A cool withdrawal. Or maybe just the stiffening of his body.

What she hadn't expected was his bark of laughter, or the way he took her hand and grinned, stage whispering to her, "I thought those plans were going to be a surprise!"

A few more ideas for the "wedding" got thrown around, including horizontally striped black-and-white bridesmaid dresses and "get out of jail free" seating cards, followed by a handful of jabs at Garrett for fooling around in the backseat of a car in a parking lot. And then the conversation shifted again and they were talking about Bethany's upcoming trip to Disney with the family, and Maeve's less entertaining travel plans for work.

And through it all Nichole sat somewhat shell-shocked by the ease with which they'd sailed through what she'd honestly expected to be the beginning of the end. Stunned to see her hand still the object of Garrett's idle touch. Startled by the revelation that this man at her side had just given her yet another lesson in the art of not taking things too seriously.

A tension she hadn't been aware of eased from her shoulders and spine, allowing her to relax back into her seat, her night and the incredible ride she was taking.

Garrett stayed the remainder of the evening, which lasted far beyond the last bite of crème brulée and through all the coffees and cappuccinos. He knew wedding talk—even in jest—was a hot button for Nichole. One that, when pushed, got her head spinning in all the directions neither of them needed it to go.

He didn't want her to worry he was running off freaked out about the mere mention of the "M" word, and he didn't want to give her the opportunity to go there herself. And once the conversation had moved on, he'd had a damn good time listening to the girls gabbing about their lives. Listening to talk spanning the spectrum from reality dating shows to mortgages to the rocky state of a mutual friend's marriage. It reminded him of when they'd all still been under one roof and he'd been privy to every inane and profound thought to cross their minds. And it was even better tonight, because intermixed with the ringing laughter he'd been hearing his whole life were the rich notes of Nichole's phenomenal laugh.

It was something he could definitely get used to, but if he wanted the chance, a little damage control was in order. And it started within a half-block of the restaurant as they walked down Randolph for some air before catching a cab.

Slanting a look at the woman tucked beneath his arm, he brought up the topic he knew had never fully left her thoughts. "That made you pretty uncomfortable tonight? The jokes about getting married?"

She glanced up at him, the relief in her eyes suggesting she'd been revving up to broach the subject herself. "It's awkward. I mean, isn't it awkward for you?"

It might have been if he wasn't with someone he knew was on the same page. "It's not a big deal. I mean, it's just talk. From my sisters. I'm used to it. But then, I've never been engaged. So I'm probably not so sensitive as you are."

There was a subtle tensing of her shoulders and Garrett knew he'd touched a nerve. "You don't have to tell me about it if you don't want to, but I'd like to know what happened."

They continued to walk another quarter of a block

in silence. Only a few cars were passing so late on a weeknight downtown.

"With Paul, I was really young and very stupid," she started. "We'd been friends since grade school and started to date at fifteen. He was the nicest boy I knew and, because we were such good friends first, when we hit the next level...the relationship kind of *took*."

Garrett nodded his understanding. Though he hadn't done much legitimate dating in high school himself, he remembered what it had been like with his friends. Oftentimes there'd been an attraction and not much else, which meant a fair amount of turnover when it came to young love. But not so for Nichole.

Because in this, like in everything else, she'd been different. Ahead of the curve.

And she'd paid for it.

"A lot of girls sort of had that wandering-eye thing. New crushes every month or so. But I liked having something steady in my life. I *liked* Paul as much as I loved him, and pretty soon we were graduating, and we'd been together for three years, and we were going to the same college. Everyone thought it was so romantic and kept asking us about whether we were going to get married. I think maybe we simply got used to the idea. Like, *Yeah, of course we will. We love each other. Why not?*" She was shaking her head then, with a quiet laugh. "Of course, the *why not* answer should have been, we were basically kids. Only no one seemed to notice."

Garrett couldn't even imagine. "What about your

parents? Didn't they try to talk you out of it? I mean what were you? Eighteen?"

"His parents thought we were a great match. His mom told me how I was like the daughter she'd never had. And my mom. *Sheesh.*" She opened her mouth, tried to find the words and seemed to fail. Then, pulling a guilty face, she tried again. "My mom is wonderful, but her priorities...her sense...sometimes it's not what it should be. She got pregnant with me when she was seventeen and my dad never married her. He basically took off when he found out about me and sent a check once or twice a year for a while. So in her book, me getting married—and to a guy she'd known forever, with us both so close at Marquette University—it was about the best news she'd ever heard."

He'd known her father wasn't around. But it wasn't until this moment he understood the extent of that absence. No father. No brother. Just a mother who'd wanted a commitment for her girl even if she was too young to make one.

Clearing his throat, he prompted her for more. "But it didn't work out?"

She shrugged. "Paul came to his senses about six months before the wedding. He was so apologetic. So genuinely sorry. He was looking around him, seeing everyone else in the world just starting their lives and figuring out who they were. What they wanted. And there we were, ready to call it done. He thought we both deserved a chance to figure ourselves out a little more. And deep down I knew he was right. So we called

off the wedding and went our separate ways. He transferred to a school out east and I got on with my life."

She didn't seem bitter. But he knew from talking
with Maeve—and from the hints he'd picked up from
her, her heart had been badly abused.

"And you met someone else?"

The way her features tightened up told him this
schmuck was someone he never wanted to meet. Con-
trary to popular belief, and with a very few exceptions,
Garrett wasn't generally a violent guy. But the pain
that flashed across Nichole's face had him wanting
to do physical harm before he'd even heard the story.

"Joel was…" She let out a sigh. "He was a few years
older. And when I met him he just struck me as so confident. Like he totally knew what he wanted—which
appealed to me, I'm sure, for very obvious reasons."

"You thought he'd be safe." Garrett gave her shoulder a rub and then stopped to take her hand in his. He
wanted to know what had happened. Wanted to see
her face when she told him.

"I'd had a couple of years to lick my wounds over
Paul, and when Joel finally asked me out I was excited
to go. Ready for something new." She slanted a glance
at him. "Ready for my mother to stop with the heavy
sighs every time I talked to her and the subtle nudges
that I should apologize to Paul—"

"What?" he barked out, but she waved him off.

"For pressuring him, or letting him go, or whatever
it was that day. Anyway, she was probably more excited
than I was when things got serious with Joel. And I

guess I didn't have enough experience to see what was real and what wasn't. Maybe I didn't want to see it because I was so hungry to build myself the family I'd wanted as a kid. Or maybe my heart just didn't have any breaks on it. Who knows? But it never should have gone as far as it did."

Garrett listened, his temper escalating as Nichole tried to explain what had gone wrong. The actions and events she'd misinterpreted. The off-the-cuff remarks she'd taken to heart. She was trying to tell him what had happened with this chump had been as much her fault as her ex's, but all Garrett could see was some spineless jackass unwilling to take responsibility for his words and actions.

"*He asked you to marry him*. After two years. How is *that* rushing or your fault?"

Nichole's skin looked pale beneath the fading light as she looked away, shame haunting her eyes. Making his gut twist for asking her.

"He said being with me was like being caught in a riptide. He didn't realize how dangerous I was until it was almost too late."

Dangerous.

Garrett's teeth ground down as he struggled for patience. Told himself not to try to look this guy up so he could pay him a visit. Have a few words.

But, damn it, what a piece of work.

When she spoke again it was so quietly he almost missed it.

"I thought we wanted the same things. That we were in it together. But I was wrong."

And though she didn't say the word he knew it was there in her head. *Again.*

Garrett gripped her shoulders, pulling her into his chest so his words would fall from his lips to her ears. "There's nothing wrong with wanting those things, Nichole. In the past, you just wanted them with the wrong guys. But you're a different woman now. With more life experience. You won't make the same mistakes. You won't get burned again."

Catching the delicate turn of her jaw in his palm, he met her eyes.

"When you meet the right guy—one who actually deserves you—you won't be too young. You won't be caught up in a bunch of empty promises. You'll be ready and so will he."

And maybe Garrett would get invited to the wedding, because even though he'd been with her like this, he couldn't imagine their not being friends when the rest was over. Couldn't imagine not being able to talk and laugh with her.

Okay, right now he couldn't imagine not being able to put his hands on her or move inside her body, but that part would go away when this thing between them finally ran its course.

Someday some guy was going to get everything he'd ever wanted in this woman. But in the here and now, at least for a little while, Nichole was his. And he was going to make every minute they had together count.

Starting right now, with getting her mind off the past by distracting her with a short-term future he'd been thinking about for a few weeks now.

"Until then..." He leaned closer to her ear, so his mouth played around the delicate shell as he spoke, effectively changing the tone of their communication within a few choice words.

Nichole's hands tightened against his chest. So sensitive.

"I've got a spectacular idea..."

TWELVE

"You can't just say *bucket list* and assume it's the end of the discussion."

Nichole was walking a step ahead of him now, laughing over her shoulder as they approached the intersection.

"Sure I can," he answered, watching with satisfaction as she turned an arched brow on him, her mind about as far from the two guys who'd torn up her life as possible. This...now...it was about *them*.

"*Sure I can?*" she demanded, that one betraying curve at the corner of her mouth spurring him on.

"Uh-huh." Reaching the corner, he moved into her space, wrapping an arm around her waist to pull her against him as he reached around her to flag a cab a block down. "You know you can't resist this face."

"Garrett," she growled at him, in a way that was more laughter than anything else.

"Nichole," he rumbled back against her ear, loving how her body almost melted into his as a result. "It's

Crush, Napa Valley. A single weekend a few months from now. I want to take you."

They'd have fun. Hit a handful of wineries. Get drunk on each other for a few nights out of town.

"Trust me, Nichole. It'll be amazing."

"I do trust you. Trusting *you* isn't the problem. It's just—"

"What? It's just a weekend. Two like-minded adults, on the same page, getting away for a little not-so-serious fun." He nuzzled her ear, catching the shell in the light grasp of his teeth for barely a second and then pulling away. "Say yes."

Her breath was soft and warm against his neck.

"I'll think about it, Garrett," she whispered as a cab slowed to a stop behind them. "How about that?"

"Perfect."

For now. He had plenty of time to convince her.

Nichole glanced at her nightstand and let out a frustrated sigh. Three a.m. and still her mind wouldn't slow down enough to sleep. And it had nothing to do with the coffee she'd had after dinner. Her thoughts had been ping-ponging around her head for half the night. Working out justifications. Trades. Negotiations with herself to ensure this tightrope of emotional investment she was walking didn't trip her up and cause her to fall.

Garrett had said they were on the same page, in the same place. And maybe if Paul and Joel hadn't come up that evening she wouldn't have thought twice...but, oh, she *really* didn't want to fall. She didn't want to be the one who got swept away. The one who cared too much.

What she wanted was everything to continue on with Garrett the way it was. Her remaining just this side of *in too deep.* The place she already stood. *Without* Garrett taking her on some romantic weekend getaway.

To Napa.

They'd talked about wine a few weeks ago—Garrett's surprise years ago on discovering his appreciation and interest in it, her curiosity about what set one vineyard apart from another, her amazement at the idea of air infused with the scent of fresh picked grapes.

And now he wanted to take her to wine country for Crush.

It would be incredible. Romantic. Fun.

They could find a little bed-and-breakfast. Rent bicycles or take the wine train. They could roll around in bed all night. Laze around through the morning.

Make love...

Sure, it was more than a few hours out with a group of friends and then a night spent getting creative between the sheets. More than laughing on her couch as they talked the night away. More than some quick kiss before darting out the door at the break of dawn to hit an early meeting. It was intimacy on an extended basis. The kind of *romantic* with the potential to rock the status quo...

Garrett understood her fears. Knew what held her

back. He'd whispered in her ear that she didn't need
to worry about their relationship going too far. That
even if she got carried away he'd keep his feet on the
ground. That she could count on him.

Closing her eyes against the yawning void of night,
she drew a deep long breath and pushed it out. Tried to
let her body go lax and find a quiet spot in her mind.
Only she couldn't stop thinking.

About the way they talked. Laughed. And played.

About how she felt when they were together.

She knew she could trust Garrett. But she was beginning to wonder if she could trust herself.

Garrett threw an arm over his eyes and let out a
feral growl.

It wasn't like he and Nichole spent every night together. They only saw each other three or four nights
a week. Okay, sometimes five. But it had become something of a standard when they did get together...they
stayed together. And he liked it.

Last night he'd dropped her at home, though, without even an attempt at going in. He'd seen that flash
of panic in her eyes at his Napa suggestion and recognized what she needed was a little time to get used to
the idea. To let it sink in that they could make plans for
a weekend in the future without the worry of it being
about *building* a future together. She needed to trust
in both of them so she could enjoy what they had to
its fullest potential.

She'd come around, he knew. But he'd figured the space would help.

Only now he'd been awake all damn night.

At four forty-five it didn't even make sense to keep trying to sleep.

On a grunt, he jackknifed up from the bed, swinging his legs over the side as he scrubbed a palm over his jaw.

How the hell was he going to make it through the day? He had meetings scheduled back-to-back until six. He'd never make it. Not like this.

If it were just the sleep deprivation he'd be fine. Hell, with the load he'd been carrying these last years he was no stranger to pulling all-nighters. But the lack of sleep coupled with this other problem—this hunger and ache that seemed to have permeated every damn cell in his system...?

Yeah, *that* was going to get in the way.

He had to do something.

Twenty-five minutes later Garrett was standing outside Nichole's door, a tray of espressos in one hand and a bag of Danish in the other. Balanced on one foot, he kicked the door—quietly. Sort of.

If she didn't answer he'd take off. Throw back the jet fuel and chow down the pastry. Head back to his own apartment and get on with the day that would have been a thousand times better if it had involved Nichole from the start.

Nichole sat up in bed, her brow furrowed as she cocked her head, listening. Because someone had just knocked on her door. Reaching for her phone, she checked her messages. Not finding any, she headed down the hall, slipping on her robe as she went.

There was only one person on the planet who would show up unannounced at the ungodly hour of five in the morning. And at that minute Nichole couldn't have been happier for the intrusion.

Maeve was just the woman to talk some sense into her. Assure her this invitation for a weekend away wasn't anything to get her panties in a twist over.

She'd tell her to relax. Settle down. Skip the theatrics and just enjoy the ride, taking it as it came. She'd remind her that neither of them was interested in something serious. So *serious* wouldn't happen.

Only she'd say it in some typically crass Maeve way that would have Nichole nearly weeping with laughter.

Throwing the door open with relief, she'd got as far as, "I love yo—" when her eyes focused on the figure that was most definitely not Maeve standing on her stoop.

Amusement tinged with confusion filled those deep blue eyes as Garrett's head cocked to the side and he asked, "Expecting someone else?"

Hand flying to her mouth, she shook her head, coughed so hard she ended up gasping and then finally wheezed out an emphatic, "Yes!"

Garrett's mouth opened, then closed as he looked off toward the sky before finally returning to her with a totally mystified stare. "Since I dropped you here at eleven last night?"

At which point she realized what she'd said and once again gave in to a fit of sputtering while she shook her head. Only then she saw Garrett was just playing with her, because that glint of mischief said he wasn't concerned at all.

And then he was stepping into her home before she'd thought to invite him, moving into her space like he knew without asking how badly she wanted him to be there. He backed her down the hall toward the kitchen, crowding her as much with the predatory intent in his eyes as the solid mass of his body. Making her come alive in a way five a.m. had never seen before.

"I thought maybe it was—"

"Yeah," he cut in, his eyes working a slow descent from her shoulders to her breasts, waist, hips, legs and toes. "I know exactly who you thought it was. The only person on the planet with the nerve to show up unannounced before the crack of dawn. My sister."

Nichole peered up at him. Sexy was radiating off his form like the rising sun. Warming everything it touched.

Sounding breathless in a way she'd only experienced with Garrett, she teased, "It must run in the family, then?"

"I wouldn't have thought so until today, but here I am."

The small of her back made contact with the island countertop, preventing any further retreat. Garrett set the tray of breakfast down beside her, then slid it away, leaving room for his hands to rest on the counter at either side of her. Caging her in.

"What are you doing here?"

"What does it look like, sweetheart?" Leaning in ever closer, so his breath played around the whorl of her ear, he answered, "I'm here for breakfast."

Taking the stairs two at a time, Garrett left the repetitive sound of hammering, power saws and the shouts of his crew behind as he ducked out in search of some relative quiet. Eyeing the progress from across the street, he dialed back his sister and held the phone to his ear.

"Sorry about that, Bethany. I'm at the Worther site today. Noisy. Everything okay?" he asked, as he always did when one of his sisters called unexpectedly.

After she'd assured him she and the kids were fine, she asked about his plans for the evening, cluing him in to the reason behind her call—though if left to her own devices she probably wouldn't have managed to spit out her actual request for another five minutes at least.

Bethany, who hated to ask anyone for anything, needed a sitter.

"I've got plans to see Nichole tonight, but I'm sure she wouldn't mind a slight change."

Bethany heaved a sigh of relief, thanking him with all the sisterly devotion reserved for sacrificial bailouts, then adding a mandatory, "Are you sure? If it's any inconvenience I'll figure something else out."

Nice offer, but she needed help. And when it came to his sisters he couldn't say no.

Or at least not when he knew they really needed it. No to a new car, to a date with the bass player from a band, a degree in basket weaving appreciation? Another story altogether.

"Not a problem. So, what time do you want us there?"

A silent beat followed and Garrett checked the phone to ensure the call hadn't been disconnected.

"Beth?"

"Um...so you're *both* coming over tonight?" she asked, in a way so the question dragged out to a point where you couldn't miss that there was way more going on than the words actually spoken.

She had a problem. But Nichole had babysat with Maeve before. Maybe even once or twice without Maeve. The kids knew and liked her.

Then he realized it might not be Nichole his sister had a problem with at all.

Just him...*with* Nichole.

Damn it, this was that Panty Whisperer bull again.

He could only imagine the rumors his sisters had heard about him over the years. What they might be spurring her on to think. Surely nothing so wholesome as making out on the living room couch after the kids went to bed? No. It would probably be some totally depraved act in the kitchen, involving half the cooking utensils. Which wasn't to say there wasn't some appeal in that idea...in his own kitchen...with Nichole the only other person in the house. But Bethany couldn't seriously believe...

"You know nothing would ever happen between us while we were responsible for the boys."

"Oh, no! Garrett, that's not what I was thinking at all. I swear," she answered, so fast and so urgently he wondered exactly how much of the sting he'd revealed in his voice. "Honey, I know you would never be anything but one hundred percent responsible while taking care of your nephews."

Garrett blinked, his mouth curving at the realization he'd just heard "the big sister voice." Something it had been the better part of two decades since he'd had the privilege of earning. *She* was reassuring *him*. Easing *his* insecurities. The novelty of it was enough to make him laugh.

"What's with that laugh?"

"Don't worry about it, Beth. Something funny from this end." True enough. He never liked to lie to his sisters. Made it a point not to do it. But the occasional dodge...that much he could live with. "So, if you're not worried about me making you an auntie again on your stairwell, what's with the drawn-out hesitation?"

She let out a laugh, again making him feel all kinds of little brother. After all these years it was a bizarre experience, to say the least.

"Well, I guess I'm a little surprised. I mean, I know you're dating, but for you to bring her for something like this...how serious are you?"

"We're not." The words fired out of his mouth, leaving a guilty aftertaste behind.

"Really? Did I just miss all the other women you've brought around to hang out with your family over the past decade or so?"

When she put it that way... Relatively speaking, this relationship with Nichole went far beyond the hookups he'd been making do with until now. But *serious* was the one word he'd had to swear to Nichole not to use. Still, the kinds of clarifications he'd have to make for his sister to understand weren't something he was up to sharing.

"Okay, yeah, I get what you're saying. But don't get too many ideas about Nichole. We're—"

"Friends with benefits?" she offered helpfully.

"No." *More than that.* "I mean, we're definitely friends too." But it wasn't like they were just a couple of pals using each other to get off. Not even close. They were more than friends, enjoying each other in an honest, open, safe capacity... They both understood, even if they couldn't quite put a name to it. They were at a good place together. A place they could both handle. "Look, don't worry about it. We're not planning to elope. And, while I honestly care about her, the only reason I've been 'bringing her around' is because she already knows you guys. I mean, hell, with this babysitting thing tonight—she's actually watched your kids on her own before. We already had plans. It would be weird not to bring her."

"Sure—no, I totally get that."

Suddenly Garrett was looking at the phone again, sliding a finger into the collar of his shirt and tugging the already open neck for more breathing room. What was with that voice? That sing-songy sort of patronizing amusement?

It was freaking him out.

"I'm serious. Look, it was an accident we even hooked up. I didn't know who she was or it never would have happened. But then it was too late. And she *does* know you. And it doesn't mean anything more than it just makes sense, okay?"

He couldn't remember the last time he'd heard his sister laugh so hard. And the sound would have been music to his ears if it hadn't so very obviously, so totally, been at his expense. To hell with this.

"Enough. Look, Bethany, we'll be there tonight. Text me the details. I've got a building to put up."

Disconnecting the call, he tried to shrug off the uncomfortable sense that despite everything he'd said, his sister hadn't heard a word.

It shouldn't matter what she thought.

It didn't matter.

Not when, for the first time in as long as he could remember, his life was exactly what he wanted.

THIRTEEN

—

Nichole wasn't sure what to expect when she walked into Bethany Slovak's home except to say she hadn't expected what she found.

AC/DC blasting at top volume and Garrett mid-jump, guitar twisted to his right as he landed in front of the TV. His nephews were squealing with delight and too focused on their absolutely *insane* uncle to actually follow the TV prompts from whichever one of those video rock band games they were playing. Or at least Garrett was playing. Sort of.

Obviously he needed some work on hitting the right notes, but when it came to flaunting a rocker attitude and entertaining his two charges...the full belly laughs coming from Neil and Norman said it all. He was a star.

Beloved.

The song ended and Garrett swung around in a showy move that ended in a deep bow toward his fellow bandmates.

But by then the kids had caught sight of her and

were running across the living room, one talking over the other as they whooped and jumped and went into a nearly impossible-to-follow account of what Garrett had been up to since he'd arrived. The rules he'd broken the last time he'd watched them...inadvertently, of course...and how their mommy had made sure to remind him.

Garrett walked over, an unholy glint in his eyes, his hair standing up in a spiky mess. "You ready to rock?"

Brows shooting skyward, she started to shake her head, but Garrett already had her hand and was pulling her over to the mic.

Nichole took one look at Garrett's tie, cinched around the stand, and laughed helplessly, "As ready as I'll ever be."

God, he was fun.

Too many songs later, her voice had taken on a two-pack-day rasp, suggesting Garrett's declaration it was time to wind down with a story had come at the perfect moment. Heading to the kitchen, she got a glass of water from the tap as Garrett settled in the center of the couch, one boy on either side, and read from *The Chronicles of Narnia.* His voice was low and clear. His audience—all three of them—were held utterly rapt.

It was...beautiful.

When the chapter was through Garrett closed the book, smiling indulgently as the boys pleaded for a few more pages. But Garrett was no lightweight when it came to kids and quickly the boys were helping to put the room to rights. Their uncle reminded them to be responsible for their toys, to respect their mother and not expect her to pick up their things, assuring them they were growing up to be men he was proud of. He shook their hands and they glowed under his praise as he pulled them each in for a hug and secured their promises they would do something silly the next day and not grow up too fast.

It made her heart ache and her throat burn in a way that had nothing to do with belting out eighties rock ballads at the top of her lungs and everything to do with the man in front of her with his nose in those little boys' hair and all that incredible, undeniable love filling the space around them. And that was when the ground beneath her feet began to give. When the world around her shook. And the status quo didn't just rock, but crumbled beneath the wave of emotion crashing over it. Catching her unprepared and dragging her back to sea with it.

Was this the riptide Joel had compared her to?

The current so stealthy and strong that once caught within it, escape was nearly impossible?

It had to be, because within the span of one man voicing his hopes for two others she'd gone from relative safety to in way too deep. And despite all Garrett's good intentions, she was afraid not even he could pull her back from the depths to which she'd drifted. *She loved him.*

When teeth were brushed, one more drink taken and the last trips to the bathroom made, Garrett tucked the boys in while Nichole waited downstairs on the couch.

She was holding it together—because this wasn't the time or place for a discussion about the state of their relationship or what this latest emotional revelation meant for it. They would see the night through, talk and joke, and she would soak up every last minute of this easy time together before it came to an end and the tough decisions had to be made.

Garrett walked into the living room and sank into the cushions beside her, letting out a thoroughly whipped breath as he did.

"I think they're down for the count."

It looked like he might be too.

"You're a very sweet uncle," she offered, wanting him to know how she saw him. "Those boys are lucky to have you."

He gave her a lopsided grin that faded as he met her eyes. "I'm lucky to have them. I didn't always appreciate it."

"But you do now?"

He nodded. "When I first heard Bethany was pregnant and then that she was expecting twins, I was... overwhelmed by their existence. The idea of them alone scared the hell out of me."

"Oh, Garrett."

His head rocked back against the cushions and he closed his eyes. "I look at them now and I'm ashamed to think back to that time. I just... Hell, Nichole. There was already so much. It's no excuse. But I felt like I was drowning. All the time. For years. Forever fighting to get my head back above water, hoping for one more gasp of breath to get me through whatever crisis or crossroads or challenge we were facing. Each night thinking just a couple more years until Maeve's out of school, or Erin's finished with her nursing degree, or Carla's married. I was counting down my list of responsibilities and suddenly there were two more getting added on. They weren't even brand-new yet. Barely more than potential. And all I could think was I wasn't ready to start the clock again with another twenty-two years on it."

Nichole leaned into him, resting her head on his chest, silently telling him she understood. Didn't judge him.

Garrett stroked a hand over her hair, playing with a curl at the end before circling back to stroke again. "It doesn't feel that way anymore. The day the boys were born I went to the hospital to check on Bethany. See the little people she'd created. And all it took was one look. Love at first sight. They were miracles. Those ugly, crinkled-up faces were about the most beautiful things I'd ever seen."

Even with her heart breaking, she couldn't help but smile at the awe behind Garrett's words.

"It was crazy. I mean there they were, completely helpless. Their mother gorked out on whatever painkillers they'd given her following the C-section and all I could think was they would be fine. Ned was so proud. Such a *dad*. He looked like he could have taken down a hundred of me if I'd gotten in the way of the little family they'd built."

"You didn't feel responsible for them?"

At that Garrett let out a short laugh. "I felt responsible, all right. I mean what if something happened to Ned? To Bethany? Trust me, the *what ifs* are infinite. But I didn't mind. I loved them. Which meant all those things I was going to have to do to feel like they were protected the way I needed them to be...were things I *wanted* to do. Couldn't wait to do."

The steady beat of Garrett's heart sounded beneath her ear. Constant, like the man who housed it.

Once he gave his word, his protection, his love...it was forever. No wonder he guarded each so fiercely.

Nichole blinked, her body going still as a sudden thought whirled through her mind. He hadn't thought he was ready to love those boys...but he did. Without reservation.

What if she hadn't been the only one caught by surprise? What if now that Garrett had had a taste of what their being together was like he could embrace it and make room for one more in his heart? His future?

It was possible.

Yes, they'd agreed not to get serious, and she'd certainly tried to adhere to the plan...but the chemistry, the way they connected....

He'd promised he wouldn't let her get too deep, but she was miles from shore. Maybe it was because he'd been caught in the same current and they were truly in this together.

Swallowing past that surge of hope, she tried to stay calm. To rein herself in enough so she wouldn't betray everything she was thinking.

"I know you're still just getting used to your freedom, now that you've finished school and your sisters are all on their own, but when you look ahead do you think you'll ever want a family for yourself?"

Garrett let out a long sigh, then shifted lower on the couch, pulling her with him as he did.

"I don't know, Nichole. A part of me feels like I've already raised four daughters. I've stayed up nights worrying about them. I've been their hero, the bane of their existence and everything in between. I've sweated with them over test scores and been as proud as a guy could be when I got to see each one of them graduate from college. And putting them first was something I was happy to do. But now that they're older... Honestly, the idea of doing it again...*choosing* to make that commitment...*asking* for another responsibility. After all the years of living with the fear that I was going to drop the ball—and it would mean the difference between a future the girls could look forward to and no future at all—I just don't think I want to go through that again."

So much responsibility for one man. "I can't even imagine what it must have been like. You were basically thrust into the role of single parent for four teen and pre-teen girls while you were still a kid yourself. But you did it, Garrett. You kept your family together and every one of you is a success in your own right."

Garrett leaned close to her ear, teasing. "A sign I should stop while I'm ahead, not get greedy and press my luck, huh?"

He was joking, but Nichole couldn't smile. A desperation was coming alive within her that wouldn't allow her to let the subject drop until there was no question left. No uncertainty surrounding what was *possible*.

"But what if you met someone you didn't want to live without? Someone who could be a partner to you? So you weren't in it alone?"

Her breath held as Garrett seemed to ponder. Finally, he simply answered, "No, Nichole. It's just not what I want."

FOURTEEN

—

Nichole sat at the edge of her loveseat, shoes on, ready to walk out the door. As ready as she'd been for the past hour. As ready as she could be when everything inside her was begging and pleading that she reconsider. To give it just a little more time. To pull back, draw a new emotional line in the sand and give herself another week of pretending she could keep her heart in check before giving up to inevitability...there was no coming back from the place she'd gone.

And in that place she was alone. Because Garrett had kept things casual from his end. Staying true to their agreement in that regard at least.

Now she needed to get out before she got hurt any worse than she already was.

Forcing her fingers to open, she pushed slowly to a stand. Put one foot in front of the other until she found herself locking her door. Then stepping into a cab. And finally arriving at the restaurant.

Before she'd even paid the driver Garrett was there

on the sidewalk, waiting for her with that big body, easy smile and ready arm.

So considerate.

Attentive.

Lovable.

Stepping into the warmth of him, she felt the first crack in her defenses. And when he pulled her into the hold of his body she almost crumbled.

She drew a deep breath, looking for strength, but found instead the clean scent of Garrett.

She should have broken away. Only knowing this was most likely the last time she'd feel his arms around her, smell the spice of his skin, take the heat of his body within her, she couldn't do it. For one minute she burrowed closer. Drew deeply through her nose and only exhaled with the greatest reluctance.

"Hey, you okay?" came the muffled sound of Garrett's voice as it whispered through the curls atop her head.

He had no idea of the havoc he wreaked within her.

Her palms flattened against his abdomen, absorbing the feel of the ridged muscles beneath even as she turned her face into the center of his chest, whispered a kiss against the spot that protected the part which wouldn't ever be hers and stepped back.

"I'm fine," she said, pushing a smile to her lips. "You want to go inside and we can get a drink?"

Arm still snug around her, because even though he didn't love her he loved the intimacy of contact, he said, "They're holding a table for us—"

"I'd rather just get a drink if you don't mind." She sounded tense even to her own ears, and Garrett picked up on it immediately.

His eyes narrowed, the skin across his cheekbones going taut, but he led her inside regardless.

Moments later they were seated at the end of the bar. A vodka tonic sweating condensation down her glass. She shouldn't have ordered it. Wouldn't have more than a sip or two. But she needed something to occupy her hands while she did what she needed to be done.

Garrett should have known something was going on. Nichole hadn't spent the night with him after they'd left Bethany's, offering an excuse about early meetings and being exhausted. He'd seen the tension in her face, felt it beneath his hands as he held her close. But he'd accepted it as fatigue, followed her home and kissed her goodnight at her door.

Only now the work day was done but the tension remained, and Nichole wanted a drink rather than dinner. It didn't take a genius or even someone with a shot glass full of relationship experience to recognize that whatever was up was about them.

Damn it.

"Talk to me, Nichole."

On her barstool beside him she closed her eyes and drew a deep breath. And then she was angling toward him, an expression on her face he'd never seen before. One so completely different than anything she'd shown him in the past, if he hadn't been sitting right beside her he might not even have recognized who this woman with the fixed semi-smile and shuttered eyes actually was.

"What we've had together these last few weeks has been incredible. Something I could never have anticipated or recognized was missing from my life. But, Garrett, neither of us were thinking it was going to be forever. And I guess what I'm saying is I think maybe it's time we end things now."

He nodded—but to himself, in a general confirmation of *yes, it's about you, Garrett*—and for a second those emotionless eyes staring boldly at him registered relief. But her relief was to be short-lived, because he wasn't about to agree.

"What's this about, Nichole? Of course I get this isn't forever. But why end it now?"

The rising din of the busy restaurant and bar gave Nichole a short reprieve in which she cleared her throat and searched every corner of the establishment like she was going to find an answer tucked behind a spare chair or potted plant. But Garrett wasn't going anywhere, and when the next lull came and her eyes drifted back to his he was still there, waiting. Holding his mounting frustration in check with the mental assurance this wasn't any big deal. Because there was no reason why something so good as what they had should end.

And he wasn't about to let it.

"Did something happen I don't know about?" Something with his sister? With Nichole's work...? Maybe they'd had a misunderstanding he hadn't even noticed. He was a guy. Apparently that sort of thing happened with them.

"No. It's not any particular thing. No incident. It's... gone on long enough, I think, if we plan to end things on a good note. You know?"

Garrett rubbed a hand over the back of his neck, wondering if more practice in the dating arena would have better prepared him for a conversation like this one. Because as it stood it didn't make sense. "Nichole, so what you're saying is there really isn't any problem. You aren't mad at me for forgetting a somehow significant anniversary or because I didn't call when I said I would. The attraction and connection are still there. This is just about ending 'on a good note'?"

The stiff set of her shoulders said it wasn't.

"It's about this getting more serious than it was supposed to," she said, her tone level and too cool for what was coming out of her mouth. "I care about you, Garrett. Maybe too much. Enough that what we have doesn't feel casual and safe to me anymore. It feels... like more than we agreed on."

She seemed relieved to have the words out, but his heart was starting to pound, the rush of blood was coming loud past his ears. This wasn't what he wanted. What either of them wanted.

She was scared. And with her past, with those guys leading her on and then letting her go, he couldn't blame her. But he wasn't going to do that. He wouldn't give her false expectations or promises he couldn't keep. All they needed to do was... Hell, they needed to get out of here.

With a nod at her glass, he asked, "Are you going to drink that?"

"No."

Garrett pulled a couple bills from his wallet and flagged the bartender before tucking them under his glass. Then, turning to Nichole, he held out his hand. "Come on."

Outside the restaurant he looked up and down the street, trying to get his bearings in a neighborhood he knew like the back of his hand but was too damned frustrated about what was happening with Nichole—scratch that—what *wasn't* going to happen with Nichole—to be able to bring into focus.

"Thank you for understanding, Garrett. Especially because of Maeve, it's important to me that we not let things get tense between us."

Understanding? Not really. And as for tense...seriously?

This was what he'd heard the guys grousing about over the years. This was the kind of *unreasonable* behind those baffled looks he'd never truly understood. But now he wanted to call up his friends from ten years ago and tell them he felt for them.

Because this sucked.

"Okay, so I'm going to catch this cab..."

A red awning halfway down the block caught his eye and he remembered parking in front of it. Great.

He took her hand.

"Garrett, wait. What are you doing?"

Looking back over his shoulder at Nichole, who he was basically towing behind him, he answered, "I'm taking you home. I get why you wanted to have this conversation in a crowded bar, but I think the least you can do is give me the courtesy of a private conversation. Fair?"

She blanched at the harshness of his tone, but he wanted her to care and he wanted her to know, without question, he did too.

"Fair." The single word came grudgingly, but he'd take it.

"Look, let's save it until we get back to your place. I don't want to do this on the street or while I'm driving."

At his car, Garrett helped Nichole in and then closed the door behind her. Rubbing the back of his neck, he figured he had ten minutes before he got her back to her place. Ten minutes to figure out how the hell he was going to fix what had inexplicably gone wrong.

Twelve and a half minutes later Nichole was ahead of him at her door and Garrett had a plan. He watched as she slid the key into the lock, turned the knob and swung open the door. Waited until she'd stepped inside and turned to him, probably with some sort of invitation he wasn't interested in hearing or willing to limit himself to poised on her tongue.

Moving into her instead of around her, Garrett

slid one hand to her waist and the other into her hair, catching her lips open. Her quiet gasp of surprise was arrested and her body without defense—he kissed her. Angling his mouth over hers and sinking into the kind of contact that had never been in question between them.

Reminding her of just one of the reasons she didn't want to end what they had. The one that, for her, had brought them together in the first place.

And she remembered, because her body was suddenly melting against his, her head falling back to grant him more access to her kiss, her hands caught in his shirt and then moving up to his face.

He wanted to press her hand more firmly to his cheek. Hold her there and just—just *be*. But he couldn't stop. Not yet. He needed her breathless. Desperate. Aching for what she could only get from him.

And then, as he gave it to her, he'd tell her she didn't need to worry. Maybe a little *serious* wasn't so bad. What they had—this kind of connection and fun and feel-good—was something they should hold on to until the very last.

Until Nichole was at a point where she was ready to move on with the white picket fence life she should have been living for years already. Or until it stopped feeling good and being everything that made him wonder how the hell she could be trying to walk away.

Hot tears pushed at her eyes as her throat tightened around all the things she didn't want to say. Everything Garrett didn't want to see...refused to understand.

"Please," she begged, her fingers already curled into his hair.

"I don't want to stop, Nichole. And I can hear it in your voice, in your breath...you don't want me to stop either."

It was true. She didn't. She wanted him to take her body. Make it his own. She wanted him to break down her defenses with his hands, his mouth and most of all his heart. She wanted him to want more than an affair.

Because *he'd* made her want more.

Only Garrett wasn't interested in the kind of *more* that would put this relationship back into a balance she could live with. Which meant as much as she might *want* the feel of his mouth on her neck, his hands pulling at her clothes, tightening over her hips...she couldn't have it.

So she uncurled her fingers from those silky strands of his hair, worked them between them and pushed.

"No."

It was a word she knew he would respect. Would never press. And, to her relief and heartbreak, in an instant he'd stepped back so the only contact that remained was where his fingers lightly grasped her own.

"Nichole. Don't do this." Dark eyes met with hers, frustrated and intense. "What we have is good. It doesn't have to end."

She shook her head, staring at him as the first tears

slipped past her lids. "How can you look at me and even say that?"

"Because it's true! Okay—I get it. You feel like things have gone further than we planned and it scares you. So—fine, we slow down a little and—"

"It didn't work, Garrett. I tried to slow down but it's not enough. You're right about it being good. It's so good between us that it's started making me want more than I have."

His eyes held hers—but she could see the shift in them. "What kind of more?"

It was a different kind of tension from simply not wanting to lose her. Telling.

"More than the promise we *won't* have a future. That you'll *never* look at me and think, *I want her. I want it all.*"

Garrett stared down at her, his expression turning hard. "We talked about this. From the start. You *understood.*"

"I know that!" she answered hotly. "Like we talked about *you* keeping *me* from getting in too deep. But even with our eyes open—" She shook her head. "It's time we take a step back."

The muscle in his jaw flexed and for a moment she thought he would continue to disagree. Maybe it was that she hoped he would.

But there was no revelation on the horizon. No argument or silent assault. Just Garrett's slow nod. "Okay, Nichole. I get it. And…I'm sorry."

Yes. Sorry. So was she.

Dropping a kiss at her cheek, he murmured. "Take care, sweetheart."

FIFTEEN

A week would have been too soon, so Garrett gave it ten days before venturing out with Jesse for a night of laughs at The Second City. Sam had organized the group, and Nichole loved improv, so Garrett figured it was a safe bet she'd be there. He wasn't disappointed. Walking through the doors, he caught sight of her tumble of red-brown curls across the room and let out a breath he hadn't realized he was holding.

The days had been crawling by since he'd walked out of Nichole's apartment. The nights even more so. And, while he understood the romantic element of their relationship was going to have to be over, he was ready to resume their friendship. Because, *damn*, he missed her. Missed the talking and laughing and the having someone who got what he was saying. People went from friends to lovers and back all the time. Without the sex clouding it up they would too.

Waving a greeting across the room, he shrugged out of his coat and started across the floor. Jesse hit him with a nod, and a few others turned around with smiles. But it wasn't until Maeve mouthed his name that the one he'd been waiting for turned, revealing those big brown eyes of hers filled with anxious trepidation.

She didn't need to worry.

It wasn't going to be awkward or tense. He wouldn't let it be.

When he met the group he exchanged a few back-slaps, knuckle-bumps and shoulder-claps before pulling Nichole in for a one-armed hug that lasted just long enough to emphasize genuine caring without pushing past platonic.

Because he was totally on board with them being friends. No matter how good that all too brief instant when her body had pressed soft and sweet into his had felt.

"How've you been, Nichole?" he asked, dropping his arm and taking a step back.

Not weird at all.

She swallowed, her eyes shifting restlessly around the space before meeting up with his. "Good, thanks. I wasn't expecting to see you."

Okay. A little weird.

"Last-minute thing. I've been caught up at the office, hammering out a new contract. Good to be busy, but I'm definitely ready for a break. A few laughs, you know."

"Sure, of course."

It wasn't going the way he'd seen it. Nichole was

wound tight and suddenly he felt like a heel having come. With a nod toward the bar he rested a hand at her elbow, leading her a few feet off from the group.

"It's okay that I'm here."

The words hadn't even passed his lips before he realized his phrasing alone had made what should have been a question more of a statement. He didn't want her to say no—apparently enough that he didn't actually give her the option to.

Nichole's eyes went wide. "Oh, no, Garrett. I mean, yes. Of course it's okay for you to be here. I didn't mean—" She broke off, glancing briefly away before turning back to him with an apology in her eyes. "You caught me off guard, is all."

"I should have called to let you know I was coming."

She glanced from Maeve back to him. "We're adults. It's not a big deal."

This time her smile was more genuine and Garrett felt himself relaxing into the idea of this new phase in their relationship. "Great. How about I go grab us a drink?"

"What do you mean, you aren't coming?" Maeve demanded through the line, her voice low as though she were trying not to be overheard.

Which was why Nichole had texted her in the first place with the news that she wasn't going to make it to Bethany's barbecue. She'd been hoping to avoid a discussion altogether, but then thirty-seven seconds after hitting "send" her phone had started its little jitterbug, announcing Maeve's call.

"My car didn't start this morning so I have to take it in."

"You're a liar."

"No." Yes. A total liar. But to Maeve, today, she wasn't about to own up to it. "I'm thinking maybe it's the alternator, or maybe—"

"Or maybe you're bailing because of Garrett. Again."

"Nope."

"You told me it wasn't going to be weird, Nichole. That what happened with you guys wasn't going to get in the way of the rest of our lives."

Guilt twisted through her belly. "It's not. I just...."

What could she even say? She'd believed it at the time. She simply hadn't known.

Nichole stared out the window at the sunshine streaming down for the first time in days. It was perfect weather for a barbecue, and she'd have loved to see everyone there. Everyone except Garrett.

Only that wasn't true. She wanted to see him...no matter how it hurt.

It had been nearly a month since they'd broken up, and she'd seen him five times. That first night had been a shock, to be certain. But after she'd been prepared for the possibility of his showing up. Ready for it. What she *hadn't* been prepared for was how difficult being friends was when her heart wanted so much more.

Garrett only had to enter the room and her body

temperature rose, everything within her tuning in to his frequency, subconsciously seeking out any hint that maybe she'd been wrong and he'd changed his mind about the idea of a future.

But nothing had changed. Because, God, she was never enough. Not for Paul. Not for Joel. Not even for her own father. Why would it be any different with this man who had warned her from the first what his limitations were?

Garrett was as comfortable as ever. Casually at ease. Attentive—albeit in a platonic sense. He'd make his way over to where she was, check in, exchange a few words before moving on to catch up with everyone else. And if that was where it had ended she might have been fine. But throughout the evening somehow he always gravitated back to her. Leaning in to share some private joke or quiet insight. Sitting closer than her heart could stand because it wasn't quite close enough. Touching her elbow or the small of her back as he passed, oblivious to the destruction those unconscious intimacies caused her.

"Look, Maeve, I'm going to have to miss today. I don't have a car, so please give Bethany and everyone my best."

"You sure you want to stick with that story?"

"Positive."

"Fine. Garrett'll be there in ten minutes to pick you up."

Garrett turned the key, listening to her car start smoothly for the fifth time in a row. He'd already been under the hood. Had her start it while he listened and looked. And he was getting ready to call his mechanic to come pick the damn thing up and see if he could figure out what was wrong.

A prime example of why it never paid to lie.

"It was probably just a fluke. Really, I'm sure the car will be fine."

Garrett looked out the open door at her. "You're sure?"

Her eyes skating away inevitably shouted all kinds of guilty, but she couldn't look at him as she flat-out lied for about the sixtieth time that day.

The door shut behind her and she figured Garrett would suggest they get a move on if they were heading out to Bethany's. She'd have to ride with him now. Her car was "unreliable." And he was here.

They'd be alone together in an intimate, enclosed space for a minimum of twenty minutes.

Involuntarily her mind wandered to the time they'd spent in cars before. When he'd pulled over with a gruff curse after her flirtations had pushed him to the breaking point. The fogged glass. The occasional law enforcement officer's intervention.

With a firm shake of her head she reminded herself it wasn't going to be that way again.

"There's nothing wrong with your car, is there?"

Time to cut her losses. She shook her head.

He stuffed his hands into his jeans pockets, staring up at the cloudless sky. "Any chance this was some elaborate ruse to get me alone?"

She stared, and after a beat he glanced back at her and then tapped his cheek. "Red."

"I wanted to avoid you."

"You may need to reconsider your approach. I've got this borderline personality disorder when it comes to damsels in distress."

Taking her hand, he rubbed her knuckle with the rough pad of his thumb. "How about you tell me what's going on? I think we're friends enough we can handle the truth between us."

Nichole let her gaze roam his face. Followed the tilt of his smile and the glint in his eyes. All of his features were working in concert to pull her in.

Even now, everything about him made her want to get closer. Made her want more than she could have.

"No," she said, slowly withdrawing her hand from his grasp, refusing to look away as his eyes hardened and the charm went flat. "That's just it, Garrett. I can't be your friend. I know you thought if we took a step back, took a few days off, it would be enough. But your friendship, your smile, your do-gooding over-protective drive are all the things that make me want more than I can have. The conversation and the laughter. The two a.m. debates. The way everything you do and everything you say makes me feel so good I can't defend myself against it."

"So you thought you'd skip Bethany's picnic today, and then what? Only go out when you know I won't be there? Is that how it's going to be? We avoid each other completely?"

The idea of not seeing Garrett anymore hurt her heart, but a part of her wished it could be so simple. Only those complications, the strings, all the obvious reasons they should have avoided this thing from the start were still there. "I don't think that's realistic or fair."

Garrett rocked back on his heels, his eyes flashing anger and shock as he demanded, "But it's what you want?"

Not even close. But what she wanted wasn't on offer. "Garrett, there's so much overlap in our social circles our paths continuing to cross is inevitable. I wouldn't ask you to stay away any more than I would want to myself—"

"So what, then?" He raked a hand through his hair, the color in his own cheeks high from the rising temper he'd never shown her before. "What do you want?"

The temper that was spurring her own.

"I want you to stop being so nice to me," she shot back, wondering how this man could refuse to see what was so completely and obviously right in front of his face. "Stop trying to whisper me into a friendship that only makes me ache for something more. Stop killing me with all your kindness. Because this show of caring—I can't take it."

Garrett's eyes were blazing, his voice going low. "I'm not trying to *whisper* you into anything."

She shouldn't have said it. Knew how it got under his skin.

But maybe that was why she'd done it. Maybe the

only way to get him to stop playing nice was if she stopped first.

And so, knowing how unfair she was being, she went on, "You haven't been trying to give me much space either."

"How the hell can you say that? The first thing I want to do when I see you is kiss you. Back you around some corner so I can show you how much I've missed having my hands on you. But I barely even touch you."

She shook her head, firing back, "You don't *get* it! The problem isn't the sex. That part I can handle fine. That part I could handle every night and never get tired of it and not worry about building unrealistic fantasies about any future we could build on how physically compatible we are together. You want to back me against a wall and push my skirt up to my waist? Fine—do it. Just make sure you walk away when you're done. It would be a thousand times easier for me than you being so damned perfect all the time!"

Instant heat flooded his gaze, but along with it came frustration. Resentment.

"What the hell is wrong with you, Nichole? You want me to *use you* and walk away?"

Her breath was coming fast, her skin hot. "Maybe I do."

Garrett's gaze darkened. "I won't."

"Why? Afraid I won't *like* you anymore? That's the point, Garrett. Even if I can't stop *wanting* you, I don't *want* to like you anymore."

His gaze darkened as he leaned closer. Close enough

so she could feel the heat pulsing off his body as well. "I don't want to be some jerk who treats you like garbage."

"And I don't want to pine away for some prince who can't stop treating me like gold but doesn't think I'm worth enough to—"

"Damn it. That's not it." Garrett's hands were hot on her shoulders, his face right up in hers as he gave her a firm but gentle shake. "You know that's not how it is!"

Nichole shook him off. "Close enough, Garrett."

SIXTEEN

—

Across the gallery, Nichole set her empty glass on a passing tray and smoothly picked up another.

She wasn't drunk.

But there was a kind of liquid grace to her movements she hadn't possessed when she'd first arrived, met his eyes for a beat and then turned away—presumably to congratulate Jesse on his latest opening. But he couldn't say for sure as he'd stayed rooted in place at the far side of the gallery.

He hadn't actually exchanged more than a cursory greeting and goodnight with Nichole since that afternoon two weeks before, when she'd basically told him the only thing he could do for her was be a bastard.

He'd been so damned mad he walked away without a word. Skipped out on his family plans and gone home to stare at the wall and swear at the empty space around him for the next three hours. That Nichole would even dare to—

Hell, he wasn't going there again.

"Excuse me...Garrett Carter?"

Garrett shifted his focus to the woman standing in front of him, a direct smile on her lips, invitation in her eyes. He tried to place her face but nothing came to him.

"Yes?"

"I thought I recognized you." She offered her hand. "I'm Fawn Lesley. Walter Lesley's daughter. You probably don't remember me, but we met briefly about five years ago, when—"

"Of course—Fawn." Her father had been putting up some luxury condos and Garrett had bid on the contract before Walter Lesley ended up backing out because of cash flow problems. The daughter must have been at one of the information meetings. "How's your father doing?"

Fawn replied that he was well, then transitioned into some light chit-chat, her hand reaching out to touch his arm in a way that was supposed to suggest an unconscious intimacy but in Garrett's experience had always been fairly rife with intent.

She was an attractive woman, by all means. Nicely built, with a sensual assortment of features. But he wasn't interested. Could barely keep his eyes on her, in fact, because they kept drifting across the room to—to where some guy was pulling Nichole into an embrace that had every muscle in Garrett's body going taut.

Not a hug. No. Not the way those arms closed around her body, almost pulling her up and in. And the extra second or six they lingered, like whoever this guy was didn't want to let her go.

Who was he?

Garrett scanned the gallery for someone to grill, but Maeve wasn't there, he didn't see Sam, and Jesse was talking to a reporter from the *Trib*. He reached for his phone, thinking Maeve did this sort of thing all the time.

He stopped to think, *Maeve did this sort of thing all the time*.

"So, Garrett—I have a confession."

He look back at Fay—no, Fawn—feeling like an ass for forgetting she was there. Nice guy. "I'm sorry? What was that?"

Lowering her impossibly thick black lashes—truly impossibly thick, because he couldn't begin to imagine what she'd put on them to make them look that way—she went on, "I had a mad crush on you that first time we met. And I know I was too young, but now...."

She let the words trail off, and Garrett pulled his mental faculties together enough to focus on what he was going to say. What he always said. Only across the room Nichole was still blinking up at the yet to be identified hugger, one hand hovering around her throat as though he'd completely caught her off guard and she was still recovering.

Damn it. Walter Lesley's girl—right. Smiling down at her, he shook his head. "I'm flattered, Fawn, but I'm...involved with someone right now."

He'd been about to give her his pat speech about

not mixing business with pleasure, ready to use his association with her father as an excuse, when he realized he had a truth at his disposal that was much more straightforward.

Nichole might have ended their relationship, but the fact that he was essentially flipping out about the guy across the room said Garrett was still very much involved. He might have stepped back, but he hadn't let go.

"Give your father my best."

And then Garrett's focus returned to where it had been. To Nichole, with her head tipped back, exposing the delicate line of her neck as she laughed at something the guy said and gestured animatedly in the air between them, pulling him in to some private joke they both seemed to understand.

Another laugh. Open. Genuine.

The riveted focus of Nichole's eyes was on this man's face like she simply couldn't look away.

And Garrett's gut took it like a blow.

Tension laced up his spine, tightening the muscles at the base of his skull, around his jaw and through his temples.

He couldn't watch this—and yet he couldn't look away.

Only he had to. Because if he sat there much longer...if he had to see the inevitable moment when this guy tested the waters with some innocuous touch...

Hell, already he wanted to take the guy's arm off and he hadn't even moved on her yet. But it was coming. Garrett recognized the signs. And God help him if Nichole moved into that touch instead of skirting away. He wouldn't be able to stand it.

And then it happened. The world around him closed in.

The blood tore past his eardrums like a freight train.

Immobilized by that single graze of some chump's fingertips at the bare skin of her elbow, Garrett couldn't do anything but wait. Watch. Stare. Until he saw how Nichole would answer the unspoken question with the language of her body. Would she move in to the touch, inviting more? Hesitate and contemplate, making herself all the more enticing a challenge and target? Or would she step back out of reach, putting up those invisible barriers that had kept her out of most men's reach for the better part of three years?

Her gaze lowered to her arm where the man had touched her. No subtlety about it. Just blatant awareness. And, God damn it, uncertainty. Didn't she know that indecision was like a red flag? A challenge. A reward not every Tom, Dick and Harry got to have.

The fingers at her elbow moved to catch her chin. Lightly, tipping her face.

The knot through Garrett's gut twisted tight. He knew what this guy was going to see in her big brown eyes. Vulnerability. Questions. Warmth and desire.

Everything Garrett saw the minute he closed his own. And now this guy—

Wasn't going to see any of it. At least not directed at *him*.

Oh, it was there in her eyes, all right. Only now her gaze had slid away from the man in front of her, was moving across the room in a slow, steady path, suggesting she knew exactly where her target lay—and had landed on *him*.

Asking if he could really let her go. Asking if he cared.

Whatever relief Garrett had felt was short-lived as frustration and hostility began to crawl up his throat.

Game-play. And he hadn't even realized she was doing it. Hadn't realized she was even capable of it.

She'd let her guard down enough to lure this sorry bastard in just to test his reaction.

See what he would do.

That was a mistake, Nichole.

She must have read his eyes, because her chin pulled back and her eyes went fractionally wider. More wary.

She'd made her point in reminding him he couldn't sleep tight secure in the knowledge that while he wasn't touching her no one else would either.

Only her little plan wouldn't work out the way she'd expected.

Across the room those deep blue eyes began to blaze and Nichole felt her skin flush at the sight of them.

The finger at her chin drifted away, along with whatever questions Nichole had about whether it was possible for her to be attracted to another man. Even a

man who'd once been her whole world. Of course looking back, it hardly seemed fair to have burdened Paul
that way when he'd been so young at the time. He'd
barely been a man at all.

Hence the broken engagement.

Just like Garrett, Paul had needed a chance to live.
Be free. But while she couldn't begrudge him the decision now, it would have been nice if he'd recognized
it before putting a ring on her finger.

"Who's that?"

Forcing her attention back to the man who, if things
had been different, might have become her husband,
she answered without pretense, "Garrett Carter."

"Carter who just put up that skyscraper down off
Wabash?" At her nod, he asked, "You two have something going on?"

She smiled up at him and, recognizing Paul for the
old friend Garrett had wanted to be himself, didn't
bother to hide the heartbreak in her eyes. "We did."

Another sidelong glance and Paul's jaw set in obvious disappointment.

"And it's not quite over," he observed. Leaning in,
he chucked his knuckles in a light graze beneath her
chin. "I know you're tough, Nichole, but if you need a
shoulder or an ear...I'd like to be there for you."

As she watched that piece of her past walk away a
low heat built at her back and her body took on a subtle charge unique to Garrett.

"Are you done?"

"It wasn't about you." The words were out before

they'd even been processed in her mind, and as soon as they passed her lips she realized how untrue they were.

She'd known he was there. Known he'd been watching her. She'd felt it as the hours passed. And though running into Paul had a been a complete surprise, and her curiosity about her reaction to him genuine, just knowing Garrett's eyes were on her throughout had made it about him as much as anything else.

Before she could admit it, Garrett's temper crackled at her ear. "Bull."

She could feel the tension vibrating between them, the hostility and accusation.

"Are you leaving with me," he growled, "or am I going to follow you home?"

She spun around to stare at him. "I don't need you to follow me home, Garrett."

With only inches between them to start, he leaned closer. "You're sure as hell acting like you need something."

Her breath caught, and then very deliberately she took a step back, and another. Turning, she muttered, "Tell Jesse goodnight for me. I'll call him tomorrow."

Returning home, Nichole didn't bother to close the door behind her after letting it swing wide enough to bounce against the far wall when she pushed through. Breath ripping in and out of her lungs, she replayed the events of the night, coloring each scene as it unfolded with what she *should* have said. What she'd wanted to scream.

He had no right!

Slapping her keys atop the bookshelf, she pinched her lips between her teeth.

You're sure as hell acting like you need something.

To hell with him.

The door closed with a hard thud behind her. The lock sounded next, putting every nerve in her body on alert. Tightening her skin, her belly.

She turned, glaring at Garrett from across the distance of her hall.

"What did you think would happen?" he asked, walking toward her as he jerked the tie at his throat until it came free.

"I wasn't—" But her denial fell short when his hands moved to his collar, opening the top button and then the next.

"You were," he answered, his voice too low and controlled to do anything but underscore the hostility surging within him. Hostility and purpose.

Another button and her heart skipped a beat, her feet starting to move in an effort to restore the space between them.

Garrett didn't hesitate to step into her space. To crowd her back into the seldom-used dining room, continuing to close in even when she had no place left to go. The thick lip of the table pressed into her flesh as her hands braced behind her.

She didn't know how far he intended to take this. What he planned to do. All she could say for certain was she couldn't look away. Couldn't say the single word it would take to make him leave. Couldn't give up this interaction that fell on the wrong side of restraint, control and good sense.

Because she was desperate for it. Starved for what she knew she shouldn't have.

"Did you think seeing another man touch you, put his hands on your body..." his palms shaped her hips and the contact was like a charge detonating deep in her belly, pushing down the line of her leg to fist the fabric and then draw it up "...would make me insane?"

The hem of her skirt rose with his hands, exposing inch after inch of her bare thighs and the pale silk of her panties to the cool air in her apartment.

"Did you think it would drive me to my knees, Nichole?" he asked, dropping to one knee and then the other without ever freeing her from the harsh burn of his stare. Making her wonder if she could ever actually be free of him at all.

It seemed impossible when, in this moment, so totally devoid of the tenderness and joy that had been a part of their every interaction, she still felt as though he owned her.

Releasing the fabric bunched at her waist, he smoothed his fingers beneath the black jersey skirt, catching her panties as he pulled them down.

"What's this about, Garrett?" Her words sounded weak and shaky. Desperate.

Exactly the way she felt.

"It's about you getting what you want," he challenged. "Isn't it?"

Before she could answer, tell him she didn't even know what she wanted, he'd brought his mouth to her, shooting sensation through that critical point of contact. The firm stroke of his tongue was shaking loose whatever fragile grasp she'd maintained on reason, lacing desire through her center, pulling the strings of her need taut and making her ache blindly for more.

Fingers curled over the edge of the table rather than through the silky waves of his dark hair, she greedily took everything Garrett gave her. It didn't matter that this need was fueled in equal parts by anger and desire, each building off the other. Or that there was no love in Garrett's eyes. That he was being cold. Callous. Proving something to her as he proved it to himself.

All that mattered was she could have him. Like this. Right now.

God damn it, Nichole needed to end this. Slap his face and tell him to get the hell out. She needed to stop him, because he sure as hell couldn't stop himself. He hadn't even realized how far gone he was until he had the silk of her skin beneath his palms and the honeyed taste of her on his tongue.

The fact that she knew exactly what was happening between them—knew this wasn't about tender affection and wanted it anyway—was all wrong. It bothered the hell out of him.

So why was he hard as a spike and letting her soft gasps wash over him again and again, hoping they never stopped?

His fingers clenched on her hips as he teased her with his mouth, let the light pressure open her to him. And still she didn't break away from his stare. Those deep brown hungry eyes—the ones he'd been certain would be the first to give—were locked with his, the desire in them obscuring everything else.

Lifting her to rest on the table's edge, he ran his hand up the center of her body and pushed her back with the steady pressure of his palm until her weight rested on her elbows and he could slip her legs over his shoulders. Leaving her open and exposed, laid out to him like a feast for his taking.

His.

Because that was what this was about.

Proving to himself that the only hands on her tonight were his. Nothing mattered beyond that one simple fact. Not game-play. Not pride. Nothing.

It wasn't Garrett's kiss she was receiving. Nothing so tender or affectionate as that. It was something else altogether. Something that had to do with power and control. Both of which she'd already given over.

It was a claim. One she greedily accepted in exchange for the scrape of his evening stubble rubbing rough against her inner thigh. *Heaven*.

His mouth moved over her. Licking. Tasting. Teasing with the barest hint of teeth until she was writhing beneath him, her breath ragged and frayed. Then, covering that achy spot of need, he drew against it with a steady, rhythmic suction more about the destination than the journey getting there. It was so good. But too fast. Too much... Not enough. Already she was coming apart.

"Garrett!"

The last wave of her orgasm subsided and, tugging at his hair, she urged him higher with a breathless, "Please. All of you."

It was only sex. She knew that. But she wanted the completion of union she'd ached for every night. Wanted the heady rush of his body moving within her. She wanted the slickness of his shoulders beneath her palms and the coarse groan of his satisfaction against her neck. The pounding of his heart echoing through her own.

She wanted him to crawl over her and push inside. Take what he needed. What she wanted him to have.

Only he'd turned to stone. Gone rigid. Immovable.

Head down now, he was no longer looking at her. Still, without seeing his eyes, she could sense the tension in him.

"Garrett?" she started, suddenly feeling more vulnerable and exposed than she'd ever been before.

She wanted to cover herself, though she knew Garrett was no longer looking. Didn't want to see her.

"Could we talk—?"

"Goodnight, Nichole."

And though he walked out without another word the message couldn't have been more clear. He'd just given her a lesson in meaningless sex. And the way this felt she'd never need another.

SEVENTEEN

—

First jealousy. Then shame. And now, as if the past two days hadn't been shaping up to suck enough, Garrett was topping them off with a solid helping of guilt.

"Her fiancé?" A string of hot vulgarities spilled out of his mouth, and even after he'd realized they were pouring straight into his little sister's ear he couldn't manage to curb them.

That explained the familiarity he'd seen. The intimacy. And, hell, even the questions in their eyes.

This was the guy who'd been Nichole's first...*everything*. Her first boyfriend. First kiss. First lover. First fiancé... First broken heart.

And he'd been little more than a kid through it all. Which meant as much as Garrett didn't want to be able to relate to that feeling of having bitten off more than he could chew...he did. He understood how a kid could have someone as incredible as Nichole ready to offer him her forever and not be able to take it.

Only Paul wasn't a kid anymore. And, thinking back to the night at the gallery, Garrett was pretty sure he'd seen all the familiar shades of longing and regret in the guy's eyes as he followed Nichole's every word, laugh and move.

"Ex-fiancé. But, yeah. And F.Y.I. he was asking Sam about her after you guys left," Maeve sniped. When he didn't offer whatever threat of beat-down she was looking for, she let out an irritable huff. "Maybe you missed the subtext of what I was saying? He's interested in Nikki. The guy she once told me would probably have been the one if she'd met him ten years later. So what are you going to do about it?"

Garrett raked a hand through his hair, looking out the window of his office at the darkening sky.

What *was* he going to do? Get lost in work for a while—like the next month or so—however long it took to get past this situation with Nichole. To stop wondering when he'd be able to see her next. What she'd think of some development at work. How hard she'd laugh at the tasteless jokes he'd picked up at the site. He needed to get past that place where so much of what he looked forward to was tied to her.

Because it wasn't fair to hold on to her when all he could offer was less than she deserved. When she'd *let him* offer her so much less than she deserved.

"I'm not going to do anything. Nichole and I are through. It's up to her if she wants to give this *Paul* another chance."

"You're through?" Another huff—this one edged with a growl. "You're a jackass, Garrett."

Totally. Without question.

But he was through being a bastard. Nichole might have thought it would be easier, but he'd barely been able to stomach himself. He owed Nichole an apology, but every damn time he got near her it seemed he took something he shouldn't. So, rather than using this as another excuse to get into her space, he was going to give her what she'd been asking him for for over a month. He was going to get out of her life for real.

The fact that they'd left things on such a foul note... Well, it just meant it would be easier for her to put him out of her head and move on with the life she was supposed to have.

When Garrett didn't turn up at her door the next day or the day after that Nichole realized he wasn't coming back. That this time it was truly over between them.

She should have been relieved. Maybe she was. Only it was hard to identify much of anything beneath the ache in her heart.

After a couple of weeks of carefully avoiding the topic of her brother, Maeve had let it drop that Garrett hadn't been out since that night at the gallery either. Though her friend had simply meant to let her know it was safe to get back in the water, Nichole had taken no comfort in the assurance.

Garrett had built a life around sacrifice and putting

his responsibilities before himself. He'd missed out on so much already. Just when he'd found his way back to his friends, to the kind of full life he'd been missing all these years—she didn't want him to give it up for her.

It was time someone else made the sacrifice so Garrett didn't have to. She'd moved on with her life before...found a new path when she'd needed to. She could do it again.

The twins' birthday was the typical run of insanity Garrett had come to expect over the years. The boys were jacked up on cake and presents and what was probably going on their fourth glass of chocolate milk. Bethany's mother-in-law was in the living room, narrating a digital slideshow chronicling the boys' lives from news of fertilization through their soccer game the week before. Garrett sat through it each year, but today it was more than he could take.

It had been a month since that last night with Nichole, and instead of it getting easier with the passing of time her absence from his life had become a hole in his chest...growing bigger every day. Numbing all the parts of him that were necessary to live.

This morning he'd woken with the absurd notion he might run into her tonight. He'd shaken the idea off immediately. In all these years she'd never been invited. And, though she'd become closer to all his sisters over the past months—even if Bethany had asked her to come—from the scant intel he'd gathered, she'd gone off the grid completely. Yet somehow he'd retained a shred of hope, because upon arrival the first thing he'd done was walk through the place, scanning each room as he went.

Now, an hour in, he was trying to keep up the façade of easygoing uncle... But the second the boys were distracted by a new guest's arrival it fell away. He needed to get out of there. Needed to walk outside. Get some air. See the sky.

He needed to breathe and it just didn't feel like he could.

Walking through the party, he looked for his sisters—only to discover they were conspicuously absent. What the—?

The laundry room? One of Ned's relatives had probably made a crack about Bethany's nacho dip and the rest of the Carter girls were talking her down from the ledge.

Following the hall behind the kitchen, he saw the door to the little room was closed but an inch gap of light showed at the base. It was quieter here, allowing him to hear the murmur of voices from within.

Busted.

Swinging the door open with an intent to rib his sisters about hiding during a family event, he didn't even make it a step into the room before a single word stopped him in his tracks.

"Pregnant—"

Whispered by Maeve and left hanging when all four of their faces swung around to his, eyes wide in varying degrees of fear and horror.

Pregnant.

Time seemed to stall as a slow burn worked across his chest, pins and needles of sensation spreading through organs that had gone numb but were suddenly alive.

The air whooshed into his lungs as he grabbed Maeve's shoulders with shaking hands.

"She's pregnant?" he demanded, a thousand things running through his head at once. Volvos and car seats, savings bonds and swing sets. A house with a yard and a fence and a back porch where they could watch the kids play while the sun set in the background.

What if something happened to her? What if they made a family and—God—what if she was taken away? If he lost her? What if he had to hold this tiny, precious little life that was Nichole's legacy in his clumsy hands and he was alone?

His gut clenched hard, but then he thought of those big brown eyes looking across the pillow at him each morning.

What if he didn't have to do it alone? What if this time it was Nichole standing beside him through the good times and the bad? Laughing with him. Letting him hold her.

Another gulp of air. This one deeper than the last.

What if this was everything that mattered?

"Garrett, just calm down," Maeve pleaded, her eyes darting nervously back and forth.

She didn't get it. She didn't need to be nervous about

him finding out because with lightning clarity it struck him that he was—

"You need to listen. Everything is going to be fine. She's going to marry him and—"

"What?" His vision pushed in, going tunnel. The only thing he could see was Maeve's face, contorting from fear to confusion to...*amusement*?

She thought this was *funny*?

"Oh, my God, no, Garrett. Not *Nichole*." Maeve was really trying not to laugh now. "I'm sorry. But it's... Erin."

His chin jerked back as another set of feminine hands grabbed at his shirt, tugging him around to face his sister.

"Garrett, please don't do anything crazy. He loves me—and look!" Erin was shoving her left hand in front of his face, showing him the neat cluster of diamonds in the shape of a heart on her third finger. "We're getting married."

Leaning back against the folding counter behind him, he met his sister's eyes. Forced his head around the information in front of him that felt like too much to comprehend. "Do you love him? Really love him? Are you sure you want to get married?"

Erin blinked at him, then turned slowly to her sisters and back. "Umm...yes."

Bethany hissed something from her corner by the dryer and Erin stood a little straighter and smiled.

"Yes. Garrett, we've been talking about getting married for months, before he found out about the baby.

I guess he wanted to wait until Christmas—not because he didn't want to have to get me a ring and a present or anything, but because he thought it would be romantic."

Garrett held up a hand, almost too deflated to bear its weight. "Then, honey, I'm happy for you."

He was. It was just that for a minute he'd been happy for himself. He'd thought he had it all. And the realization he didn't had pretty well knocked the wind from his sails.

A second later the laundry room door opened again. George popped his head in, looked down at Erin's hand still held in front of Garrett's eyes, blanched and backed out with a quick slam of the door.

Garrett rolled his eyes as Maeve let out an indelicate snort. The girls started laughing, and him along with them. Looking from one sister to the next, he thought George was going to have to toughen up if he was going to be a parent. It was no walk in the park... but it would be worth it. Garrett thought about all that Erin and George were in for together and it struck him how incredibly lucky they were. How much beauty and awe lay ahead.

Then Bethany, Carla and Erin left the room, leaving Garrett and Maeve behind. His littlest sister cocked a brow at him and asked, "You okay?"

"Not yet," he answered, rubbing at that bruised feeling over his chest.

She stepped into him and gave him one of those very sweet kisses that involved tugging him low even as she stood on her toes to reach his cheek. "You did such a good job with us, Garrett. You protected our family. And, as much as I hate what you had to give up to do it, I'm thankful you did—because you kept us together. But now it's time for you to take care of yourself. I love you, bro."

EIGHTEEN

——

Nichole shouldn't have come. It was stupid and self-destructive. Equivalent to picking at the wound over her heart that already wouldn't heal. But Sam had asked her to come over for dinner, wanting to talk. And when she'd tried to make an excuse, he'd rather effectively guilt-tripped her into it with a reminder about her month-long disappearing act.

He wanted her out of her apartment.

He wanted her to talk.

And so she'd come.

But now she was sitting on the rooftop of her dreams and nightmares. The chilly October air was biting her cheeks as Sam ran downstairs to grab them a couple of mulled ciders he'd whipped up.

The sun was doing its slow decent through the western sky, coloring everything in its path. In the quiet of the evening, removed from the street level rush, she drifted back through the months to summer. To that first toes-dip back into the pool. To Garrett.

If she'd had any idea what she was in for would she have done it anyway?

Yes.

Again and again and again.

Because while it lasted it had been incredible. Amazing. And having her heart break was better than never feeling it at all.

The scrape of feet moving over the rooftop sounded behind her and a tingle of awareness skirted across her skin.

Not Sam.

Garrett.

Her breath left her lungs in a rush and her fingers splayed wide over the rail as she tried to tell herself to be calm. To be strong. But all she could think was that he'd orchestrated this. He'd gone to the lengths of pulling Sam into whatever his plan was. After all this time, maybe he still wanted something.

Stepping beside her, Garrett set two mugs of cider on the rail and then wrapped a thick blanket around her shoulders from behind, so she wouldn't have to turn away from the blazing sky before them.

His hands shaped her upper arms, but he left a space between them.

"I never should have left the way I did. I shouldn't have behaved like I had some right or claim or justification for going nuts about you talking to another man. Not when you'd offered me something so much more and I'd turned it away."

Her shoulders slumped as that crazy bit of hope she'd been clinging to slipped through her fingers.

He was here to apologize. After all this time. Because Garrett...was *Garrett*. She'd become a responsibility somewhere along the way, and he was simply incapable of not facing up to it.

"I wasn't trying to play a game with you, Garrett. Not consciously anyway. I just... When Paul showed up—"

"You don't owe me an explanation. It doesn't change what I did. I'm sorry and wish I'd had the clarity of thought to do something else."

Walk away? Maybe take that blonde who'd been flirting with him home?

She didn't want to think about that night. Right now she just wanted to remember all the things that had gone right. The fun. The ease. The promises fulfilled.

"Okay," she said, her following deep breath meant to be the break between one topic and the next. "So—been enjoying many sunsets lately?"

"I've been watching them—but, no. Not exactly enjoying them."

She turned then, drawn more by the man behind her than the star around which her very existence revolved. "Garrett, you've to got to stop holding yourself accountable for everything. If you've been worried about me—"

"I have."

This was why she was looking into accountancy

firms across the country. Why she'd set up an interview for the next week.

She shook her head, but he just went on.

"Because if you feel even half as hollowed out and lost as I do, I don't know how you're surviving." Garrett looked past her to the sky beyond and then back to meet her eyes. "I watch the sunsets I've been waiting years to be able to enjoy and all I can think is how empty they are without you. I tell myself this connection is nothing I can't walk away from or get over. But there's *nothing*—nothing about it. We have a bond, and I'm finally starting to understand just how significant it is. It's about friendship and caring and attraction and the kind of sweet insanity of need I couldn't understand until I met you. It's about me wanting you to be a part of everything I do because everything I do is about a thousand times better when you do it with me. I was an idiot for taking it for granted, selling it short. Selling *us* short. Trying to let you go and doing such a poor job I don't think I'll ever be able to forgive myself."

Nichole's hands were on his chest then, the blanket slipping off one shoulder. Garrett caught it before it fell from the other. He tucked it around her and used it to pull her close.

"Garrett, what are you saying? That you want to give this a try for real? You think you might—?" Her voice cracked and she had to stop and blink back a tear. "You might want a future together?"

The muscles of Garrett's throat worked up and

down as his jaw flexed. He gathered her hands in the warm hold of his own and held her gaze. "No. I'm saying I don't think I can live with a future where *we* aren't. Today I—I misheard something and got it in my head you were pregnant."

Nichole's chin snapped back. "Oh, God. I'm not—"

"No." He gave her a wry smile. "I know. But for the sixty seconds I thought you were...*damn*, Nichole, that might have been about the most terrifying, best moment of my life. Because suddenly I could see how incredible it was going to be...and how much there was to lose. A lifetime of everything I wanted condensed into a single minute. There was only one course of action and I wanted it. *Get Nichole back and marry her today.*"

Garrett drew a breath and closed his eyes. "But then it was over. Because it's Erin who's pregnant...not you."

He wanted her. Not some casual bit of fun. Not just the good time while it lasted. Pure elation pushed beneath her ribs as her stunned mind tripped and staggered over the words she'd never expected to hear. Processing each one until—

"What? Erin's pregnant?" She gasped, wondering if George still lived.

"Stop searching my clothes for blood. George is fine. They're getting married and I'm happy for them— mostly. But that doesn't matter right now."

She couldn't be hearing him right. Not about any of this. And especially not about his sister's pregnancy and impending marriage ranking as a lower priority than what was happening with *her*.

But that was what Garrett was saying. It was what was in his eyes. In the way he held so fast to her hands. Like he thought she might get away before he'd had the chance to make his case.

God, he was a fool.

"Garrett—"

"Nichole, all I could think when I figured out it wasn't you was *no!* Because that meant I didn't have anything to tie you to me. And I'd been such an ass I didn't know if I'd ever be able to get you to give me another chance. But I need another chance—because I swear to you, sweetheart, I can make you as happy as you deserve to be."

"Garrett—"

"And now I'm glad you aren't pregnant. But only because I want you to know this isn't just some sense of responsibility or obligation driving my actions. It's that I'm finally seeing what was in front of me the whole time—what I didn't have enough experience to recognize. I love you."

Words she'd never thought to hear. More beautiful than she could have imagined.

"Nichole, you have to—"

She was through trying to talk to him. Tugging her hands free, she reached up and grabbed his gorgeous, agonized face and pulled him into her kiss. For an instant there was only the blissful press of lips. Sweet contact and connection.

And then Garrett's arms slipped around her, pulling her into the solid strength of his body. He parted her lips with a desperate urgency that echoed her own. Murmuring her name against her mouth again and again before pulling back with a curse and looking into her eyes.

"Being without you has been the worst kind of torture. I thought I was afraid of losing my freedom, of ending up trapped in something beyond my control. But I didn't know what real fear was until I realized I'd lost the one person who makes me feel free. Alive. Complete."

"You haven't lost me. I'm right here." In the tight hold of his arms. With all that devastating blue shining down on her in a way that went straight to her soul and warmed her from the inside out. "I'm yours, Garrett."

"Then I'm never going to let you go. And I'm never going to give you a reason to want to leave, either, because I couldn't take it again. I couldn't take that feeling of being dead inside after knowing what it finally was to live."

Her palm cupped the solid line of his jaw as she peered up at him with a watery smile. Voice thick with emotion, she answered, "You won't have to."

"Promise?"

She nodded. With all her heart.

Garrett straightened, the muscles along his throat moving up and down as he swallowed.

"Good, because I love you, Nichole." Then, as if in slow motion, he went to one knee in front of her.

Her heart started to race and she shook her head

as something other than joy began to push its way into her chest.

Within the cradle of his big strong hands sat a neat black leather box opened to reveal a breathtaking diamond solitaire. "Marry me?"

"Garrett, no. I don't— I'm not—" She was terrified of that ring. Though by far the most beautiful, it was not the first she'd been offered. What if she put it on and he changed his mind again? What if they planned some elaborate wedding, invited everyone they knew, and then he woke up with the sense they'd rushed?

She couldn't take it. Not with him. Not after believing she'd lost him already.

"I won't let you down again, Nichole. If you can trust me with it, I'll take care of your heart for the rest of my life."

She looked down into those soulful eyes and realized this was no boy making a man's promise, nor some guy caught up in a moment. This was Garrett, who only made promises he could keep and who took his responsibilities more seriously than anyone she'd ever met. Garrett, who only knew how to love with his whole heart. Garrett, the man she wanted more than her next breath, who was worth any risk she had to take.

She did trust him. And he was offering her everything she'd ever dreamed of.

"Yes," she whispered, vowing never to forget the look of joy and relief spreading across his face. "I'll marry you."

He took a great breath and slid the ring onto her finger.

For a moment neither of them moved as they stared at the symbol of the commitment Garrett had just made.

"I like the look of my *forever* on your finger."

Nichole closed her eyes at his gruffly spoken words, letting that subtle distinction sink in to the very center of her heart.

Not just a ring. He was giving her a promise with no end. A lifetime together.

It was a perfect fit.

"I do too. It's beautiful, Garrett."

Pushing to his feet, he wrapped one hand around the small of her back, pulling her flush against the warm heat of him. When his mouth met hers it was in a kiss as soulful and lingering as his promise of forever.

When the kiss ended he pressed his forehead against hers. And then, cupping her jaw in his big hand, he said, "So, we've got a few hours... I didn't know if you were going to agree, or if I was going to have to try to whisper you into it, but we're booked on a flight for Vegas tonight."

At her shocked expression he let that half-smile of his crook its finger at her heart. "What? You didn't think I'd give you a chance to change your mind, did you? We might have missed the sunset tonight, but I want you wearing my name before sunrise tomorrow."

"I love you," she whispered.

That wicked smile fell from his lips, leaving nothing

but the stark honesty of his answer. The promise she could believe in. The future they would share.

"I love you too."

* * * * *

Available July 23, 2013

#25 GIRL LEAST LIKELY TO MARRY
The Wedding Season • by Amy Andrews

Samuel Tucker is the last person scientist Cassie Barclay would ever date—after all, he seems to be the true definition of all brawn and no brain! But when it comes to the bedroom, it's Tuck who can show Cassie a thing or two! Can he convince her that love and sex have nothing to do with logic and everything to do with chemistry?

#26 FAKING IT TO MAKING IT
by Ally Blake

Nate Mackenzie has a plus-one dilemma for his mate's wedding. So discovering that Saskia Bloom has to do online dating research for a magazine, he strikes a deal. He'll give her all the research she'll ever need—and she'll be his fake date for the wedding. But despite their obvious sexual attraction, they're complete opposites in every way. Can they be at all convincing as a harmoniously happy couple...?

#27 ALL BETS ARE ON
by Charlotte Phillips

Ask Alice Ford to shine in the boardroom and it's a done deal. Ask her to go on a first date and she's a quivering mess! So when she discovers that she's the target of an office bet to get her into bed, it's her professional nightmare. Office legend Harry Stephens is her unlikely savior. But what is Harry really after?

#28 LAST-MINUTE BRIDESMAID
Girls Just Want to Have Fun • by Nina Harrington

Heath Sheridan, Kate Lovat's old school crush, needs an emergency bridesmaid *and* a girlfriend stand-in, and offers Kate his business know-how in exchange for a weekend of pretense.... Limousines, stylish dresses and hot CEOs chasing after her—Kate is living her teenage fantasy! But soon she realizes that you have to be careful what you wish for—because sometimes you get a whole lot more than you expected!

———

REQUEST YOUR FREE BOOKS!
2 FREE NOVELS PLUS 2 FREE GIFTS!

HKI3

SPECIAL EXCERPT FROM

 HARLEQUIN®

KISS™

Amy Andrews brings you the next story in
THE WEDDING SEASON miniseries with

GIRL LEAST LIKELY
TO MARRY

She'd never been kissed like this.

She'd never *kissed* like this.

And still she was full of him. Her head buzzed with the essence
of him. Her mouth was on fire. Her belly was tight. The heat
between her legs tingled and burned.

Tuck barely managed to hold on to her as Cassie kissed him
as if she were an evil genius intent on wicked things and he
was her latest experiment.

He pushed her hard against the door, wanting to get closer,
to kiss her more deeply. But he'd forgotten it was already slightly
open and she stumbled backward, their mouths tearing apart.

He grabbed for her, found her elbow, then dropped it once
she'd stabilized. And then they stood staring at each other,
breathing hard, not moving for a moment, neither sure which
way to jump.

Tuck knew enough about women to know that look in
Cassie's eyes. He knew he could pick her up, stride into her
room and lay her on the bed and she'd follow wherever he
took her. And enjoy every single second of it.

But he saw a whole bunch of other stuff in her eyes, too.

HKEXP20724

Most of it he couldn't decipher. But he could see her confusion quite clearly. Obviously the kiss just did not compute for Cassie.

She looked as if she needed some time to wrap her head around it. He sure did!

"Are you okay?"

Cassie nodded automatically, but she doubted she'd ever be okay again. She felt as if she'd just had a lobotomy. Could a kiss render you stupid?

"I think I should go now. Unless…" He dropped his gaze to her swollen mouth.

Cassie shook her head and took a step back. *No unless. Go, yes, just go.* He'd turned her into a dunce.

Tuck smiled at her dazed look. It was nice to have left an impression on Little-Miss-Know-It-All. "Good night, Cassiopeia."

Cassie was incapable of answering him. She feared she'd been struck mute. As well as dumb. She watched him swagger to his room opposite, slot his key in, open his door. He turned as he stepped into his room.

"I'll be right over here. If you need a cup of *shhu-gar.*"

Cassie had no pithy comeback as his door clicked quietly shut.

Pick up GIRL LEAST LIKELY TO MARRY
by Amy Andrews, on sale July 23
wherever Harlequin books are sold.

A dilemma, a deal...a date!

AVAILABLE JULY 23!

FAKING IT TO MAKING IT
by Ally Blake

Charmer Nate Mackenzie is in the middle of a plus-one dilemma for his friend's wedding. Any of his recent dates would start dreaming of a solitaire for their own left hand. Worse, going stag will leave him at the mercy of a setup by his ever-hopeful sisters.

Discovering that Saskia Bloom is doing online dating research for a website, he strikes a deal. She'll take the research rather than a relationship and he'll get a fake date. There might be no shortage of sexual attraction between them—but as complete opposites will they be at all convincing as a happy couple...?